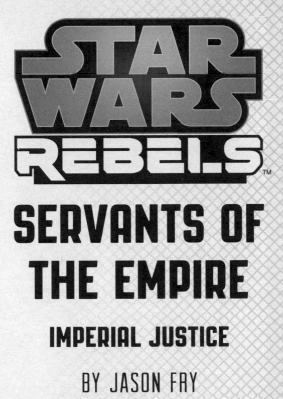

STAR WARS REBELS™

SERVANTS OF THE EMPIRE

IMPERIAL JUSTICE

BY JASON FRY

DISNEY · LUCASFILM PRESS

Los Angeles • New York

Cover illustration by David Le Merrer

All rights reserved. Published by Disney • Lucasfilm Press, an imprint of Disney
Book Group. No part of this book may be reproduced or transmitted in any form
or by any means, electronic or mechanical, including photocopying, recording,
or by any information storage and retrieval system, without written permission
from the publisher. For information address Disney • Lucasfilm Press,
1101 Flower Street, Glendale, California 91201.

Printed in the United States of America

First Edition, July 2015

1 3 5 7 9 10 8 6 4 2

Library of Congress Control Number: 2015935579

V475-2873-0-15142

ISBN 978-1-4847-1660-1

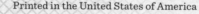

SUSTAINABLE
FORESTRY
INITIATIVE
Certified Chain of Custody
Promoting Sustainable Forestry
www.sfiprogram.org
SFI-01054
The SFI label applies to the text stock

Visit the official *Star Wars* website: www.starwars.com

PART 1:
LOYALTY

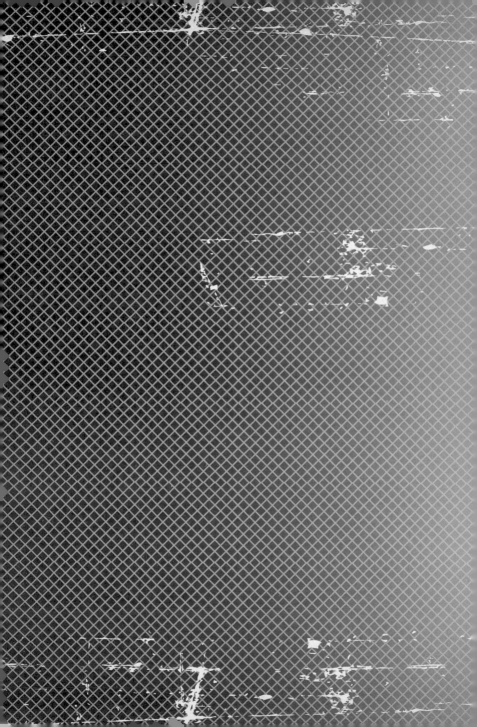

"Double-time it, cadets! *What is wrong with you this morning? Do you want to be back in your nice, soft bunks? Is that the problem, cadets?"*

Zare Leonis didn't have to peek back at Sergeant Currahee to know what she looked like at that moment. He knew she'd be red-faced and hard-eyed, spewing sweat and spit as she ran alongside him and his fellow cadets.

"Ma'am, no, ma'am!" he yelled in unison with the other young cadets of Lothal Academy.

At the beginning of the year, Zare and the others would have been gasping for air and fighting cramps, as expected for fifteen-year-olds new to the rigors of military training. But now a ten-kilometer predawn run was nothing special; the cadets hadn't even muttered objections as Currahee rousted them from their bunks in the Academy barracks to run along the road that cut through Lothal's hills.

"Does the sarge always yell like that?" asked Kabak, a newcomer to Zare's Unit Aurek with close-cropped black hair.

"Pretty much," Zare said with a shrug. "And we yell back. Lots of yelling in the Imperial Army. Better step it up, though—you and Rykoff both. You don't want to give Curry a *real* reason to yell."

Kabak and Rykoff nodded, glanced at each other nervously, and picked up the pace. Both had recently transferred from other academies on Lothal. They didn't know that Currahee's yelling was now mostly for show. The squad's weak cadets had been weeded out long before, and those who remained were both physically and mentally tough. Zare hoped that was true of the two newcomers as well—for their sakes.

"A fine day to be alive, ladies and gentlemen!" called Lieutenant Chiron, breezing by the cadets. As always, the slim, handsome officer looked like he was barely sweating.

"You know what would make this early-morning stroll even better?" Chiron asked.

"Sir, no, sir!" Zare yelled along with the cadets.

"Killing a few traitors," growled the fourth member of Unit Aurek, the sallow, grim-faced Nazhros Oleg.

"You're a lot of fun, Oleg," Zare said. "If you find any traitors while we're out for a jog in the Easthills, let us know."

Kabak and Rykoff laughed, but Oleg offered Zare a sardonic smile.

"You'd be surprised where the enemies of the Empire are hiding," he said.

Before Zare could demand to know what he meant, Chiron began to sing, and Zare instinctively raised his voice in the booming cadences of the song he'd learned on many a morning run:

> *From the razor cliffs of Mittoblade*
> *To the fire mounts of Seffi,*
> *We will fight our Empire's battles*
> *In space, on land and sea;*
> *We will strive for right and order*
> *And to keep galactic peace,*
> *On the day we claim our place*
> *In our Empire's Army.*

Zare found himself grinning as he flew along the road. It was a crisp, cool morning. Autumn would soon yield to winter on Lothal, with the grasslands fading to pale green and then yellow. He was in the best shape of his life, and he'd earned the respect of his instructors and his fellow cadets . . . well, except for Oleg. But then, Oleg's dislike could be considered another badge of honor.

The cadets reached the top of the hill that marked the highest point in the Easthills, and they hooted happily: from then on they'd be running downhill. Chiron grinned at Zare, who touched his knuckles to his forehead as the cadets began to sing the final verse:

> *A salute to you from these cadets*
> *Assembled here to serve;*
> *In many a fight we'll show our might*
> *And never lose our nerve.*
> *Oh, we'll lay them low from Old Lettow*
> *To distant Gardaji,*
> *Our every story told for the glory*
> *Of our Empire's Army.*

"Cadets! Sound off!" Currahee bellowed.

"Huzzah!" Zare yelled back with the others.

"I can't hear you!"

Zare started to yell, but the sound died in his throat as he rounded the bend.

He should have been looking out over the Lothal plains toward the spires of Capital City, the grasses below him undulating like the surface of a great ocean, broken by scattered hillocks resembling islands. But that familiar view was gone. For nearly a kilometer, the grasses had been burned away and the land ripped open. Massive construction droids clawed at the dirt, with metal pillars rising into the air behind them. Welding droids zipped back and forth on repulsorlifts, their torches brilliant sparks of light.

Zare stopped short and Oleg nearly collided with him, squawking in protest.

"What you're seeing is a new BlasTech weapons lab," Chiron said, gliding around Zare with his usual annoying grace. "It'll open by spring. The Emperor has chosen Lothal for another key defense facility—which means more jobs and industry for the planet."

Chiron smiled and ran off. Smoke drifted over the cadets. It was acrid, and Zare coughed, his eyes watering.

"*Is this nap time, Leonis?*" demanded Currahee.

"Ma'am, no, ma'am," muttered Zare, running to catch up with the others.

And to think a moment earlier he'd been happy. The

Empire hadn't changed; it would despoil and destroy the grasslands in the same way it had ruined the orchards where his friend Beck Ollet had once lived—the same Beck Ollet whose failed rebellion had ended with his vanishing into Imperial custody.

And, Zare remembered with a shudder, the Easthills was where his sister, Dhara, had disappeared the previous spring. The Empire insisted she'd run away from the Academy, but Zare and his girlfriend, Merei Spanjaf, had discovered otherwise. The truth was that Imperial agents had kidnapped Dhara because she was Force-sensitive. They had taken her to the planet Arkanis as part of a secret program called Project Harvester.

Zare had enrolled at the Academy to discover what had happened to Dhara, posing as a model Imperial cadet even while he worked to assist the Emperor's enemies. He'd helped his fellow cadets Jai Kell and Dev Morgan escape after the Empire identified them as Force-sensitive. Zare had pretended to try to stop Dev and Jai, and his efforts had been convincing enough to win an Imperial commendation. Only Oleg seemed to have suspicions about what had really happened that day. But then, Oleg was suspicious of everybody.

Zare had nightmares all too often, and usually the bad dreams involved a fellow cadet discovering he was a traitor, the Empire's dreaded Inquisitor arriving to interrogate him, or a communiqué arriving to say his sister was dead. But there was another fate he had to guard against: what if he played the role of perfect Imperial cadet so well that he forgot it was an act?

The construction site below them was just the latest wound inflicted on Lothal by an Empire that intended to use the planet up and abandon it. Cadets Kabak and Rykoff were replacements for Force-sensitive boys who'd barely escaped the fate of Dhara Leonis. And the hills around Zare were where the Empire had stolen his sister from her family.

Zare would be the best cadet on Lothal, get promoted to the officer-training program on Arkanis, and find Dhara. And then, once his sister had been rescued, he'd help the enemies of the Empire bring it crashing down around the evil men and women who had built it.

Those were the important things—not patriotic songs, or the good regard of Chiron and Currahee, or making friends with the next generation of Imperial officers.

Zare shook his head and picked up the pace, giving Kabak and Rykoff a grim nod as he ran past them. He wouldn't forget again. He *couldn't* forget again.

★ ★ ★

That morning the cadets didn't run back to Capital City for roll call and their usual regimen of classroom instruction. Instead, Chiron directed them to one of the many fields the Academy used for training exercises—a grassy expanse broken up by clumps of shrubs and out-croppings of rock. The grasses were pale with dust that blew ceaselessly from the hills in the west during the winter, irritating people's eyes, noses, and throats.

"Line up by units," Currahee said, and the cadets quickly and efficiently sorted themselves into quartets, with Zare and his three fellow Aureks at one end of the field, followed by units Besh, Cresh, and Dorn, and the all-female units, Esk and Forn. On the edge of the field waited a quartet of trainers in crisp olive-green uni-forms and gray field armor.

Zare heard the whine of repulsorlifts approaching, and an Imperial troop transport came to a smooth halt in front of the cadets, who tried not to blink and cough as its engines sent whirlwinds of dust spinning among them. Six stormtroopers disembarked from the craft's side compartments, regarding the cadets from behind their featureless white helmets. Once they had assem-bled, an officer emerged from the passenger cab of the transport. He had close-cropped dark hair and wore a captain's rank badge.

Zare stiffened at the sight of him. Piers Roddance

knew Zare's parents slightly and had attended the parties the Leonises held for their children's acceptance into the Academy. But Zare knew he was no friend of theirs: Zare and Beck Ollet had watched from hiding as Roddance's stormtrooper unit broke up a peaceful protest by farmers in the Westhills the previous summer. Many of the farmers had died or disappeared, and the Empire had covered up the incident.

Roddance took his time stripping off his black gloves and eyed the assembled cadets. His eyes lingered on Zare, who forced himself to stare back without flinching.

"Today's exercise will demand your best, cadets," Roddance said in the clipped tones of the galaxy's Core Worlds. "To begin, let's review how to advance on a position—in this case, one held by a high-value target. Though today it would be more accurate to say 'a very low-value target.'"

He smirked and nodded to one of the troopers, who strode over to the back of the transport. A protocol droid stepped out of the vehicle, looking alarmed. He was an older model, metal coverings dingy and pitted.

"How may I serve, sir?" the droid asked Roddance uncertainly, brushing at a loose wire hanging from his midsection.

"Like we all do—by following orders," Roddance

said, gesturing to the troopers. They hustled the old droid across the field, his gyros whining as he struggled to keep pace.

"You've drilled in the basics—select a route or axis of advance, seek cover or concealment where available, and never block your squadmates' covering fire by crossing in front of them," Roddance said. "Troopers, begin exercise. No comlinks—coordinate using hand signals only."

The stormtroopers darted across the field—one pair to the left, one pair to the right, the remaining two kneeling and firing at potential enemy positions. Zare admired the speed and efficiency of their movements and the way they signaled to one another. In less than thirty seconds, two troopers converged on the droid and aimed their E-11 blaster rifles at his chest.

"Oh my—I surrender!" the old droid said plaintively, struggling to lift his arms.

"Eliminate target," Roddance said, and the droid vanished in a fusillade of shots. One of the troopers kicked at the droid's head, which rolled across the field, photoreceptors still flickering.

Roddance grinned.

"These older-model droids were judged not worth the expense of refurbishment or resale, but they can still be of service," he said. "Don't worry—you'll get your own targets to practice on. Get your gear and assemble your rifles. The exercise begins in five minutes."

A pair of bulky labor droids emerged from the transport carrying crates, which they set down in front of the cadets before being led away by the stormtroopers. Zare watched them go for a moment, then shook his head. It was time to assemble his blaster.

"Oh no, everybody—Leonis is *sad*," Oleg said with a grin as he slapped a power cell into his E-11. "Look at him. He's going to cry over some junky old droid that was nothing but a waste of power."

Kabak and Rykoff looked up as they strapped on their field armor. Oleg was rubbing his eyes with his knuckles, pretending to blubber.

"Shut up, Nazhros," Zare said, using the first name he knew Oleg detested.

"Make me," Oleg said.

Zare's fury boiled over. He crossed the space separating him and Oleg in two strides, grabbed a fistful of the other cadet's shirt, and yanked Oleg toward him.

"My pleasure," he snarled.

Then Currahee was between the two boys, shoving them apart.

"In front of the captain?" she demanded, eyes bulging with anger. "That's three demerits each. And I'll have all four of you in the hangar at 0400 tomorrow for laps."

Rykoff groaned. Zare waved his hand dismissively at Oleg.

"Suit up," Currahee barked. "Coordinates for the exercise are loaded into your helmets' nav units, so get them hot. Leonis, you're squad leader. Oppo force is three trainers. Review the terrain holo on the way to the coordinates. And, gentlemen? You've exhausted my patience for the morning. One more screw-up and I'm going Base Delta Zero on this unit. Do you want that, Unit Aurek?"

"Ma'am, no, ma'am!" Zare roared as he lowered his helmet's faceplate.

Thirty seconds of the field exercise was enough for Zare to push the confrontation with Oleg out of his mind and sink into the familiar rhythms of figuring out routes to objectives and spotting likely hiding places for opponents. He and Kabak flushed out one Imperial trainer and drove him into Oleg and Rykoff's sights, where Oleg popped him with a sting bolt. They then navigated a tricky dogleg where Zare was certain the two remaining trainers would try to catch them in a crossfire. But they made it through without incident, and Zare found himself peering across a rocky field toward a large boulder screened by shrubs whose leaves had turned a glossy red and orange.

Zare raised his faceplate.

"Our objective's behind that boulder," he said to the other three cadets. "I'm thinking they'll have one trainer guarding the target, with the other covering that open space on the left—probably from concealment up there. Oleg, break left and try to draw their fire—we'll make sure they keep their heads down so you and Kabak can get to the target. If you get pinned down, we'll move to flank them."

"You're thinking I'll get killed, Leonis," Oleg sneered, "so you can win the exercise."

"I'm thinking that you're the best marksman in the unit—if you take down the trainer on the left, we can go around that boulder in pincer formation," Zare said. "Now, if you're done worrying about yourself, let's go accomplish this mission."

Oleg scowled and lowered his faceplate, nodding curtly at Kabak. Zare and Rykoff did a low crawl through the grass to an outcropping of rock and peeked over it. The boulder was about ten meters ahead. Zare flipped his helmet's visual filter to infrared. He couldn't see a heat signature among the shrubs.

"Tell the other two to move forward on the count of three," Zare said to Rykoff, who started to scramble up to one knee to make the necessary hand signals.

Zare shoved him back down.

"Either you'll get shot, or they'll see the signals and we'll *all* get shot," he said. "Use your flasher. You know flash code, right?"

"I think so," Rykoff said.

"By next exercise you need to *know*," Zare said sternly.

But Rykoff was just nervous. He detached his flasher from his utility belt and blinked out a message to Kabak, who acknowledged it.

"One, two, *three*," Zare said, then got to his knees alongside Rykoff, white sting bolts spraying from their E-11s. Oleg erupted from the underbrush, firing wildly as he sprinted for the boulder, with Kabak laying down covering fire.

"Flanking maneuver, *now*!" Zare said.

He hurdled a tumble of rock, trusting Rykoff to keep up with him. Oleg crowed and an Imperial trainer got morosely to his feet ahead of them, rubbing at his stomach where Oleg's training-intensity bolt had hit home.

Zare waved frantically at Oleg, hoping his meaning was clear: *Celebrate later. There's one more out there.*

"Double-time it!" he told Rykoff, racing for the boulder.

A sting bolt struck Oleg in the helmet, wreathing him in white sparks. Kabak hit the dirt, but Zare was already dashing around the boulder from the other side. The trainer was in front of him, facing the other way with his blaster raised. A droid stood next to the man.

"Got you, sir!" Zare said, leveling his blaster at the man's back.

The trainer turned, scowling beneath his field helmet, then holstered his weapon.

"Thanks for not taking the shot, kid," he muttered.

Zare nodded; he knew a sting bolt burned for a good half hour.

He turned to regard the droid representing their high-value target and felt his heart flutter. It was a nanny droid—a newer model than his own family's Auntie Nags, but one with similar synthflesh arms and gentle facial features.

"Hold your fire—no one's given us orders yet," he reminded Kabak and Rykoff, then switched his comlink to external mode. "Squad leader, the target is secured."

"Please don't deactivate me," the nanny droid said, wringing her synthflesh hands. "I have spent twenty years caring for children at the Education and

Economics Ministries. I know some of my systems need replacement, but I assure you my critical programs are all in perfect order."

"Transmission acknowledged, Unit Aurek," Currahee said in Zare's ear. "Stand by."

Please don't give me the order to fire, Zare thought. *Please not that.*

"Take the target into custody, Aurek," Currahee said a moment later.

Zare exhaled in relief.

"Stand down," he told the other Aureks, holstering his blaster.

"I would gladly assist a newer model," the nanny droid pleaded.

Zare and the other cadets raised their faceplates. Oleg shook his head and winced, still feeling the effects of the sting bolt.

"Just please don't take me from the children," the nanny droid said. "I would miss them so."

"It's going to be all right," Zare told the droid, patting her shoulder.

A klaxon signaled the end of the exercise and Zare grinned, slapping hands with Rykoff. The nanny droid looked at their faces in wonder.

"Why, you're little more than children yourselves," she said.

"Good job on that flanking maneuver, Zare," Kabak said, extending his hand. "I was worried that—"

Oleg stepped forward, adjusting his blaster's controls, and began to fire. When he was done, the nanny droid's torso was riddled with smoking holes and the ground was spattered with melted synthflesh.

"What—what did you do that for?" Zare demanded.

Oleg blew on the hot barrel of his blaster.

"What do you care?" he asked, then stepped close to Zare. Kabak and Rykoff watched in shock.

"You're a fraud," Oleg hissed. "We both know it. What happened back on the walker, the day Morgan and Kell escaped?"

"You read the report," Zare said. "Kell stunned the driver, then you. Then he overpowered me."

"Yeah, I've read that bunch of poodoo. So Kell beat three-to-one odds and then fled with Morgan in a speeder. But he didn't take the blaster. No, you wound up with that, Leonis. You had their speeder in your sights at point-blank range, but somehow you missed."

Zare tapped Oleg in the chest, hard.

"You think I don't regret that every day? I already said you're the best marksman in the unit, didn't I? Too bad you let Kell jump you, or maybe you would have been able to take the shot instead of lying on the deck unconscious."

"You're lying," Oleg said. "I know it. And one of these days, I'll prove it."

Roddance walked around the boulder and looked down at the smoking remains of the nanny droid.

"Who destroyed this target?" he asked. "There was no kill order for this unit."

"Cadet Oleg did," Zare said. "On his own initiative."

Roddance looked at the cadets, then shrugged.

"Saves us the trouble of a disassembly order," he said with a grin, then turned away.

"Sir!" Oleg called, hurrying to catch up. "I wanted to ask you a tactical question."

As the two walked away, Oleg turned and offered Zare a sardonic grin. Zare felt sick to his stomach. He knew what Oleg suspected. But how many of those suspicions had he shared with Roddance?

Merei Spanjaf knew her father was trying to be nice—and that he was genuinely concerned.

"We're worried is all, Mer Bear," he said, using his old pet name for her. "Your grades are down, and that's not like you. We just want to know what's wrong."

Merei lowered her eyes, reminding herself not to give in. Yes, Gandr Spanjaf just wanted to know what was wrong. But Merei's mother, Jessa, was watching, and her gaze was level and hard. Jessa wasn't one for talking things out. Once she knew what was wrong—or thought she did—changes would be made in the Spanjaf household.

Merei reached for the tongs and put another helping of redsprout on her plate, careful not to seem rattled.

"Like I told you, nothing's wrong," she said after a bite. "V-SIS is a new school, and this stuff's hard. That's one of the reasons I've been getting together with the guys in the anti-intrusion club before school."

"I hope this isn't about boys," Jessa said.

Merei's fork hit the table with a clatter.

"There's only one boy, Mother. His name's Zare, and you know I only get to talk to him three times a week for fifteen minutes at a time."

"Nobody's accused you of anything," Jessa said.

"Doesn't sound that way to me."

"Whoa, whoa," Gandr said beseechingly. "We just want to help, Mer Bear."

"Then let me figure this stuff out. On my own."

They ate without speaking for a few minutes, the only sounds those made by utensils against plates. Merei wondered what would happen if she told her parents the real reason her grades were slipping: she'd infiltrated the Empire's data networks by leaving snooper programs lying around the Transportation Ministry, then created a fake Imperial identity with good enough security clearance to access the files that revealed what had happened to Zare's sister.

Merei's snooper programs had been set to erase themselves, but a fault in a ministry computer had let an Imperial anti-intrusion team recover one—and the head of that team was none other than Jessa Spanjaf. Merei knew her mother was an exceptionally good security investigator, and she feared it was only a matter of time before Jessa tracked the intrusion to her own household.

And what would that mean for her family? Merei couldn't make her mind go there. It would be the end of everything—she knew that much.

"Anyway, how's your investigation going, Mom?" she asked, trying to sound casual.

"You need to worry more about school and less about my job," Jessa said.

Gandr glanced at his wife, frowning.

"Your job is what I want to do," Merei said. "I've learned as much from the two of you as I have at school."

Jessa looked at Gandr, then sighed.

"Fine. We're investigating everything we can at the Transportation Ministry, since that was the site of the initial breach. We're examining the snooper program the intruder used and trying to match its code to work done by known criminal programmers."

"Any clues?" Merei asked, feeling her stomach knotting. The snooper had been programmed by someone working for Yahenna Laxo, the head of the small-time criminal organization called the Gray Syndicate.

"No clues yet, but we're still looking," Jessa said. "The cam feeds from the Transportation Ministry had been recycled by the time we discovered the break-in, so there's no footage of the intrusion. But we found a woman who says she bought raffle tickets that day from a Phelarion School student named Kinera Tiree."

Merei nodded, remembering the Imperial bureaucrat who'd stopped her just as she was exiting the ministry.

"Phelarion?" Gandr asked. "Isn't that the fancy school for government kids?"

"Yes," Jessa said. "And there is a Kinera Tiree who goes there—she's the daughter of the education minister. But we showed the woman who bought the tickets an image of Kinera, and she swears it's not the same girl. And the real Kinera Tiree was taking an exam at the time."

"But whoever sold the tickets was able to impersonate her," Gandr said. "Which means the intruder was a teenaged girl."

"Most likely," Jessa said.

"It could have been a shapeshifter," Merei said. "There are species that can assume other forms, right?"

"A few," Jessa said. "But Imperial intelligence keeps a careful eye on any shapeshifters with underworld ties, and it doesn't know of any that are unaccounted for locally. So we're starting with the more obvious possibilities. Our witness is pretty useless—she has the brain of a bantha calf—but we're planning to show her images of every Phelarion student. If that doesn't turn anything up, we'll have her look at the pictures of every schoolgirl within a hundred kilometers of Capital City."

Merei must have looked startled, because her mother caught her eye and smiled thinly.

"There's something you can tell your instructors at V-SIS," Jessa said. "Showing pictures to a witness may not sound very high-tech, but most of the time, we find intruders through old-fashioned police work. Keeps us out of the courts and builds a more solid case."

Merei nodded gravely, but she was only half listening to the rest of the conversation. She was trying to figure out how many students about her age were in Capital City and its surrounding towns, how many pictures a day her mother's investigators could show their witness, and how quickly she'd be identified.

She did the dishes and climbed the stairs to her bedroom, where she stared at her homework until her datapad chimed, reminding her that Zare's free period at the Academy was beginning.

When Zare commed her, though, she immediately noticed something had changed: he was in a featureless cubicle instead of the office belonging to Minister Tua, where communications were unmonitored.

"Hey," Zare said with a smile, but his eyes were filled with warning. "It's a lovely night here in the Academy barracks."

Merei understood immediately: they weren't free to talk openly.

"With all the recent . . . unrest . . . things must be different there for you," she said.

"A little bit," Zare said. "But don't worry. The tighter security procedures are here to protect all of us."

Merei nodded, thinking that they both had been involved in that unrest and were now victims of their own success. Because they'd helped strike a blow against the Empire, they could no longer talk to each other the way they had.

"We're doing a lot more drills," Zare said. "Drills and field exercises. Nothing too tough, though. So tell me about school."

Merei told him about some of her classes, trying not to let her frustration show. She couldn't tell him what was really happening any more than he could; if anything, it was worse, because Zare didn't know that Merei's break-in had been discovered, or that she was being pursued by her own mother.

Merei ran out of meaningless things to say, and they stared at each other miserably for a few moments.

Merei's datapad chimed. Someone else was comming her, from an ID she didn't recognize. She scowled and flipped the new transmission over to her message queue.

"Winter break's only a couple of weeks away," Zare said. "It's not so long."

"I know," Merei said. "But suddenly it feels like forever, somehow."

They said their good-byes, and Merei stared at her datapad's blank screen for a long moment. Her message indicator was blinking, alerting her she had audio waiting.

She opened the message and sat bolt upright as the voice of Yahenna Laxo emerged from her datapad.

"Got some homework for you," the crime boss said, sounding pleased with himself. "First thing tomorrow, same classroom as last time. And this homework is mandatory. I'd hate to see such a promising student spend a long time in detention. See you soon, kid."

Merei erased the message and forced herself to breathe. She'd almost convinced herself that Laxo had no use for her and wouldn't try to collect any debt beyond the credits she'd paid him for the snooper program. But she should have known better. Now she was being hunted on two fronts.

Zare knew he was in trouble, because it was Roddance who got him out of his bunk, shining his datapad's task light into Zare's face. The Imperial captain had remained stubbornly silent as Zare asked frantically what he'd done and where he was being taken.

Their destination was Roddance's office, and as soon as the black door retracted into the wall, Zare saw who was waiting for him. It was the Inquisitor, the Imperial agent who'd interrogated him after Dev Morgan's escape. He sat behind Roddance's desk, a simple drinking cup on the desk in front of him, and smiled pitilessly as the still-silent Roddance shoved Zare forward.

"Last time we met, Cadet Leonis, you told me your sister wasn't dead," said the Inquisitor, his yellow eyes like burning coals. "You told me you knew that. That you'd always been able to sense her."

Zare's instincts screamed for him to run. But he had nowhere to run to. Even if he could get away from Roddance, there was nowhere on Lothal where he'd be safe from the Inquisitor. Perhaps there was nowhere in the galaxy.

"Watch carefully, cadet," the Inquisitor said, stretching out his hand. The cup jiggled on the desk, then rose smoothly into his hand. The Inquisitor took a sip, his eyes blazing above the rim. Then he set the cup down and smiled at Zare.

"Your turn, cadet," he said.

Zare shuffled forward reluctantly, his knees wobbling and twitching.

"What's the matter, cadet?" asked the Inquisitor. "Lifting the cup is the simplest of tasks for one who can feel the Force. I can do it. Dev Morgan can do it. Your sister, Dhara, can do it. Now it's your turn. Go ahead, Leonis."

Zare's hand was shaking as he lifted it from his side.

"You made me think you could feel the Force," the Inquisitor said. "I believed you. Now prove it."

Zare remembered how the decoder had risen from Agent Kallus's desk to where Dev had been hiding in a duct above. He willed the cup to rise and cross the empty air to his hand, trying to block out the Inquisitor's terrible smile.

Nothing happened. Zare tried until the sweat stood out on his forehead and his arm was tired. The cup remained motionless on the desktop.

The Inquisitor leaned forward, white teeth gleaming in his gray face.

"*Liar*," he whispered. He got to his feet, the chair scraping across the floor behind him . . .

. . . and Zare woke up with a gasp.

The barracks were dark, the only sound the breathing of the other cadets, asleep in their own bunks. Zare sat up, half convinced he'd see Roddance standing nearby, but the ruthless captain was nowhere to be found.

Zare dropped to the floor, landing silently beside the bunk where Kabak lay sleeping. The floor was chilly beneath his bare feet. He padded down the hall to the bathroom and got the water as hot as he could stand it. He splashed it on his face, then stared at himself in the mirror.

His sister had been alive when the Inquisitor questioned him after Dev's escape—he knew that much. Zare had taken an awful risk by telling the dreadful being he could feel Dhara out there somewhere, calling to him: if Dhara had been dead, the Inquisitor would have known immediately that Zare was lying, and would have wondered what else he had lied about.

Which means I'd be dead now, too, Zare thought, blinking at himself in the harsh light of the bathroom.

But that didn't mean Dhara was still alive. He'd asked Merei to use her forged Imperial credentials to check on Dhara's status, but she'd said it was too dangerous now, and the obvious alarm on her face had made him reluctant to push her.

Zare closed his eyes. He thought of his sister: of the curve of her face, and the way her smile slipped from sardonic to genuine, and the rising sound of her laughter. He imagined his mind traversing the hyperspace lanes between Lothal and Arkanis, searching for his sister's mind. He thought of his voice amplified a millionfold, calling out among the stars. He tried to attune his ears to her voice, to her thoughts, so he'd be able to capture the smallest whisper.

But there was nothing—nothing but a teenage cadet standing in a harshly lit bathroom in the middle of the night.

All at once Zare felt a surge of anger rip through him. It wasn't fair. Why had Dhara been given the gift of the Force and not he? Imagine all the things he could do if he had the abilities of the mysterious Dev Morgan.

An absentminded cadet had left a toothbrush beside

one of the sinks. Zare stared at it, then raised his hand. He ordered the toothbrush to fly to him, then closed his eyes and tried again. His hand remained stubbornly empty.

Zare opened his eyes and caught sight of himself in the mirror, standing there with his hand raised. He looked ridiculous—like he was imitating one of the statues outside the abandoned Republic Senate Building, the ones that supposedly personified freedom or perseverance or the pioneer spirit.

He shook his head and laughed, then stopped. He had no feel for the Force, it was true. But that wasn't something to be sad about—because if he could command that strange power, he'd have disappeared, too.

Zare padded back to the barracks and his bunk, starting awake seemingly a minute later to the martial music of reveille and Currahee's barked orders. He put his uniform on sluggishly, scarcely aware of what his hands were doing, and trudged with the other cadets to the assessment hall, where Commandant Aresko and Taskmaster Grint awaited them. Behind the two Imperials stood Roddance and Chiron.

"Squad NRC-077 for your inspection, Commandant," Currahee said.

"At ease, cadets," Aresko said. "After winter break

you will begin the next phase of your training—assisting with Imperial operations here on Lothal."

A murmur of excitement rippled through the ranks, dissipating as Currahee bellowed for silence.

"Since arriving at this academy, you have all been tested," Aresko said. "Some of your colleagues have proved wanting, and are no longer with us. Those of you who remain will soon be selected for more specialized training. Some of you will be assigned to assist our brave stormtroopers, with the hope that you will earn the right to wear their armor one day."

That's an honor I'd rather skip, Zare thought, remembering his neighbor Ames Bunkle and how his time at the Academy had changed him, seemingly draining his individuality away until he was little more than a number.

"And some of you will be evaluated for officer training," Aresko continued. "But all of you will undergo testing to determine your fitness for Imperial service."

The commandant's expression darkened.

"The reputation of our academy has been damaged by regrettable recent events, which necessitates this testing," he said, his eyes roaming over the cadets standing at attention. "You will be questioned about your own conduct and that of your fellow cadets. The truth—whatever it is—shall make our Empire stronger. No cadet who is loyal and pure of heart should fear what lies ahead. And of course none of you are to blame for having offered the hand of friendship to those who betrayed our Emperor."

Aresko's eyes lingered on Zare where he stood between Kabak and Oleg. Zare forced himself to stare straight ahead.

As far as he knows, you're a hero, he reminded himself. *You received a commendation. Don't be afraid.*

But an icy prickle traveled up his spine anyway. What if the Empire had discovered something? What if the Inquisitor had sensed Zare's deception, or Dev had been captured and confessed Zare's true role? What if a trap was closing around him even as Aresko spoke?

Zare steeled himself to remain expressionless and still as Aresko concluded his remarks and dismissed the cadets. But as they turned to the left to march away, Oleg leaned forward to whisper in Zare's ear.

"You're going down, Leonis," he said. "Now they're going to find out *everything.*"

Merei was shivering when Laxo's decrepit speeder van pulled up to the abandoned repair ship on the outskirts of Capital City. She checked the lock on her jump-speeder, wrinkled her nose at the five-eyed alien driver, and rapped impatiently on the craft's rear doors.

They opened with a groan of distressed metal to

reveal a Rodian female, with crimson spikes crowning her head, and two evil-looking human men. The Rodian was pointing a blaster at Merei.

"Hoped I'd never see you again," she grumbled.

"And good morning to you, too, Rosey," Merei said, clambering into the passenger compartment and sitting on the metal bench before the other two thugs remembered they were supposed to search her.

The speeder van made a series of turns meant to confuse her sense of direction, rumbled across the city for a while, then came to a halt with a sigh of repulsor-lifts accompanied by an ominous orchestra of clanking and clattering. Down a filthy alley was a metal door that led to the kitchen at the rear of Laxo's headquarters. The place had once been a tavern but was now crowded with network terminals. A few humans and aliens were sitting at the terminals, typing and guzzling caf. On the other side of the room, a trio of Laxo's thugs were playing sabacc while another four slept, snoring wetly.

One of the young men behind a terminal was Jix Hekyl, her classmate from V-SIS. He'd introduced her to Bandis Yong, who'd connected her with Laxo's organization. Apparently Jix had decided to do some work for the crime boss himself.

The blue-skinned, yellow-eyed Pantoran boy caught her eye, then looked away, his cheeks flushing indigo.

Merei felt her own face burning as Jix risked a shy glance back in her direction.

Merei was trying to figure out whether or not to say hello when Rosey caught up with her. She stopped short, staring at the sleeping thugs, then muttered what Merei assumed was a vile Rodian curse and pointed to the back room. As Merei climbed the narrow stairs, a startled snort sounded behind her, followed by yelling in a number of languages.

Upstairs, Yahenna Laxo was sitting behind his Imperial officer's desk, looking at the screen of a sleek black network terminal. The fleshy crime boss gave Merei a grin and waved for her to sit on the couch. The broad picture window across the room had been missing when Merei last visited; now it was translucent glass.

"Merei Spanjaf, the pride of V-SIS," Laxo rumbled, his blue eyes bright sparks in his ruddy face. He spread his arms with a grin. "Welcome back to the loving embrace of your friends at the Gray Syndicate."

Merei thought about pointing out that a handful of teenage slicers and narcoleptic guns-for-hire barely amounted to a criminal organization, let alone one that merited such a fancy name. But she settled for shaking her head as Laxo made a minute adjustment to his gravity-defying blond pompadour.

"I've been thinking about how best to make use of

you," Laxo said, and Merei bristled at the idea that she was a tool for him to employ. "I could use you as a courier, perhaps. Or to keep an eye out for Imperial agents. Or maybe you want to improve your slicing skills by breaking into new parts of the Imperial network?"

"I'm not doing any of those things," Merei said.

"Really? Why'd you come, then, if all you were going to do was tell me no?"

Merei lowered her eyes, embarrassed and angry. They both knew she had no choice but to be there and to do what he wanted: he could destroy her with a single message to the authorities.

"You know what I was doing when I was your age?" Laxo asked, tucking a stray lock back into place over his forehead.

"Combing your hair, probably."

"Ha. That's true—pretty girl like you ought to try it sometime. But mostly I was figuring out what I wanted to do with my life. So this was the problem I had to solve: the only real market for my talents as a programmer was with the Empire, but I wasn't interested in helping the Emperor spy on people and restrict their freedom. That's what the Empire's best at, you know—using the promise of security to take away rights that people took for granted under the Republic."

"So you're some kind of revolutionary, then," Merei said sarcastically. "I'm not buying it. You didn't have to work for the Empire. You could have signed on with one of the megacorporations."

"There's no difference anymore," Laxo said. "All corporations of any size are now instruments of the Empire—either they've been nationalized, or their directors know better than to cross Palpatine's bureaucrats."

Merei scowled. Most people she'd met on Lothal thought no further than their single small planet. What a waste that one of the few exceptions was a selfish lawbreaker like Laxo.

"And so your answer was to become a criminal?" she asked him.

"Seemed preferable to being a slave."

Laxo's casual impudence made Merei want to provoke him, to shake him out of his smug self-assurance.

"And what have you done with all that independence?" she demanded.

"You mean besides help schoolgirls break into Imperial networks?" Laxo asked with a grin. "Well, I take a cut from illegal betting parlors throughout Old City. I find smugglers to transport goods of various kinds, and I stockpile those goods or distribute them, depending on supply and demand. I discover information and figure out what it's worth and who'll pay for it. I help people solve problems they can't go to a legitimate business for help with. Plus a few other things. But that's it for starters. Now let me ask you a question."

He waited until Merei looked up.

"Think about the businesses I'm involved in—gambling, feeding people's bad habits, that sort of thing. Would those businesses disappear if I did?"

"Of course not," Merei said.

"Of course not. And the people who do those things— is anyone forcing them to do them?"

"No," Merei said. "But still—you profit from people's misery."

Laxo's big bright grin got bigger and brighter.

"You're right, I do. But that misery was here long before you and I were, kid, and it will remain long after we're gone. *Someone* will profit from it—why shouldn't it be Yahenna Laxo and his friends?"

"I won't do anything illegal for you," Merei insisted feebly.

Laxo put a hand to his chest.

"Merei Spanjaf, you wound me," he said with a theatrical flutter of his eyelids. "Do you think I'd ask you to do anything that would trouble your conscience?"

From Laxo's smile, Merei could guess that soon he'd do just that.

Rumors were flying long before the first cadets were summoned to interrogation rooms for questioning about their pasts.

"They're conducting interviews like this all over Lothal," said Uzall, a cadet from Unit Besh. "I heard they expelled two dozens cadets from a regional academy on the far side."

"I heard that, too," said Giles. "And that one of the cadets at Pretor Flats confessed to treason and was taken away by stormtroopers."

Zare sat up on his bunk and looked down at the cadets. Kabak and Rykoff were watching the conversation with worried expressions while Oleg reclined on his own bunk, a smirk plastered to his face.

"That sounds pretty serious, Giles," Zare said. "Who told you about the cadet at Pretor Flats?"

"My brother heard it from a friend of his," Giles said.

"Oh," Zare said. "And, Uzall? Where'd you hear about the expulsions?"

"We were talking about it in the mess hall. I don't remember who brought it up."

"You don't believe it, Zare?" asked Kabak.

"Of course I don't believe it," Zare said. "And neither should you until someone you actually know was actually there when something happened. No more of this friend-of-your-brother stuff. It's all ridiculous rumors."

Kabak and Rykoff nodded.

"But they're questioning all of us," Giles said. "They wouldn't do that if they didn't think they'd turn something up."

"Sure they would," Zare said. "They're scared because of what happened with Kell and Morgan, so they're doing everything they can to cover their behinds. No one here has done anything wrong. Just answer their questions and you'll be fine."

The cadets nodded—all except Oleg. He leaned forward, eyes glittering.

"*We'll* be fine," he said. "But how about you, Leonis?"

The other cadets looked from Oleg to Zare.

"What are you talking about?" Zare asked. He braced himself for Oleg to bring up something about Kell or Morgan, to make some wild accusation in front of everybody.

But Oleg surprised him.

"Your sister's a deserter," Oleg said. "Don't you think that should be grounds for expulsion?"

Zare slipped from his bunk in one smooth movement,

landing on the floor. He stared up at Oleg.

"Come down here and say that to my face," he said. "Or do I have to haul you out of your bunk?"

Oleg landed in front of Zare and stepped forward until they were nose to nose. Zare was conscious of the other cadets watching in fascination. His heart pounded in his chest.

"I said your sister's a deserter," Oleg hissed. "And I asked you if that shouldn't be grounds for expulsion. Well, Leonis? Shouldn't it be?"

"Take it back," Zare said. "One warning is all you get."

Oleg just smiled. A second later their arms were windmilling and they were stumbling across the barracks. Oleg smashed into the wall and hit Zare in the ear, then the cheek. Then the two boys were on the floor, fists flying. Zare could taste blood in his mouth and hear the other cadets yelling. Then they were dragged apart. Zare struggled to free himself from the cadets keeping him away from Oleg, but there were too many of them.

"What is the meaning of this?" bellowed Currahee, storming into the barracks. The cadets let go of Zare, who stared at Oleg where he stood a few meters away. Oleg's nose was streaming blood, and one of his eyes was swollen. Zare was breathing hard, and his hands

were shaking. He looked down and saw that his knuckles were bloody.

"Leonis attacked me," Oleg said calmly. "Look at me. Look at him. It's all the evidence you need."

Currahee's eyes studied Oleg's battered face, then jumped to Zare's swollen cheek and skinned knuckles.

"Is that what happened here, Leonis?" Currahee asked.

Zare said nothing, trying to get his breathing under control and stop his heart from thudding in his chest.

You idiot, he thought dismally. He'd be expelled and lose his chance of getting to Arkanis and finding Dhara.

"I asked you if that's what happened here, cadet."

"Sergeant," said Kabak, then bit his lip. "I saw the whole thing. Oleg slipped."

Currahee frowned.

Oleg looked at Kabak in fury. *"Liar! He's a liar!"*

"Cadet Rykoff?" Currahee growled.

Rykoff put his hands behind his back.

"It's just like Kabak said—Oleg slipped."

"You can't possibly believe that!" Oleg sputtered.

One of Currahee's eyebrows crept upward.

"Oh, I do believe you slipped, Cadet Oleg," she said. "On your own tongue, I suspect. You might want to be more careful about that."

Oleg looked at the other cadets in shock. Zare forced himself to remain expressionless as Currahee stepped close to him, the corners of her mouth turned down.

"But if there are any more accidents in this squad, I'll have to conduct a full investigation," she said. "Is that clear?"

"Yes, ma'am," Zare said.

Currahee nodded, gave the cadets one last look of warning, and marched away. The cadets turned their backs on Oleg. He stared at them, mouth moving silently, then wiped at his bloody nose and looked down in distaste at the red smear on the back of his hand. He lifted his eyes to see Zare watching him.

"They can lie for you here, but they won't be there when you're questioned," Oleg warned. "I know things about you, Leonis—I know what you've done. Get your story straight—and make sure it sounds better than your version of what happened on the walker."

Merei was headed downstairs, fitting her goggles over her hair, when her father intercepted her.

It was barely dawn, not the hours Gandr usually kept, and his eyes were puffy with sleep.

"Hey, Mer Bear," he said. "Another early start, huh?"

"It's the only time we can go over anti-intrusion

stuff," Merei said, feeling a stab of regret at the ease with which she now lied to her father. "But I'm learning a lot, so it's worth it."

She pressed her carryall tighter against her side with her elbow, wondering what her father would think if he looked inside and saw the quintet of thumb drives she had to deliver to Laxo's associates across Capital City.

"I want you to do me a favor," Gandr said, his lean face grave. "Take this."

He handed her a small black device on a string.

"A locator?" she asked. "I've got one built into my datapad."

"This is so we can find you if you're in trouble," Gandr said, holding up one hand. "It doesn't transmit automatically—much as it scares me sometimes not to know where you are, you deserve your privacy. It's only if you need it. This baby's military-grade stuff—the signal can get through most anything, short of a few metric tons of lead or an Imperial data center's jamming field. But then you're not likely to find yourself in one of those."

The way things are going, who knows? Merei thought, but she smiled at her father and leaned over to give him a kiss on the cheek.

"Thanks, Dad," she said. "I'll keep it in my pocket."

"And if you need it, you'll use it," Gandr said.

"And if I need it, I'll use it. I promise."

She waved to her father and left the Spanjafs' apartment, hunching her shoulders against the cold. A moment later she was racing through the quiet streets, her jumpspeeder's engine thrumming beneath her.

When she arrived at the first address on Laxo's list, she immediately checked it again. She was in a newly built, wealthy precinct of Capital City, not far from the Leonises' house. But the number was correct.

Merei parked her speeder, found the right thumb drive, and leaned on the buzzer she wanted. The cam unit above her whirred as it fixed on her face.

"No handouts, girlie," a woman's voice said peevishly. "And shame on you for asking before breakfast. Better run along before the authorities sweep you up for detention."

The cam went silent. Merei leaned on the buzzer again.

"That's it, I'm calling the—"

"Syndicate business," Merei said gruffly, remembering what Laxo had told her.

"Oh! Oh! I'm so sorry! He'll be right down! But . . . it must be freezing. Would you like some tea?"

"No handouts, remember?" Merei snapped. "Send him down."

A minute later a rotund, bald man answered the door, cinching the neck of his luxurious robe against the chill.

"You're new—she didn't know," he said apologetically. "I'm sorry."

"Forget it," Merei said, handing over the thumb drive. "He says four days."

"Four days? But . . ."

The man gathered himself and nodded, looking ashen. Merei threw him a salute as she sauntered back to her speeder.

That was interesting, she thought.

The next address was in Old City. Merei cut through the marketplace, where she found her speeder blocked by a pair of corporate bureaucrats walking in the center of a narrow alley. She crept up to within half a meter of them and gunned her engine, making them jump.

She pulled up to a rundown warehouse on the outskirts of Old City and cut her engine, looking around. A speeder parked nearby turned on its lights, blinding her, and she threw up one arm in protest.

"Whaddya want, kid?" someone said as she blinked away the spots in her vision.

"Delivery," she said, snapping her goggles down to cut the headlights' glare.

"Business delivery?" one of the beings in the speeder asked doubtfully.

"Exactly."

The lights cut off, and a bearded human got out of the speeder's passenger side, tucking a blaster back into his coat. He ran a portable scanner over Merei, then nodded at his companion.

"We'll make the delivery for you, kid," he said.

"No, you won't. Boss says I do it. Direct contact."

The man scowled and spoke into a comlink, then gestured to a narrow metal door at the corner of the warehouse. It was dented and covered with scrawled graffiti, but the lock was a heavy magnetic model and the overhead cam unit was state-of-the-art.

More here than meets the eye, Merei thought.

The magnetic lock deactivated, and the door swung open. A tall, skeletally thin Gotal stood on the other side of the door. He nodded at the speeder down the block, then turned to regard Merei.

"Kriffing Laxo," the Gotal grumbled, scratching at one conical horn. "What are you, ten? Can never tell with your species."

"I'm fifteen," Merei said.

"Glad he's amusing himself. You have something for me, or did you come to play tooka dolls?"

Merei handed over the thumb drive, and the Gotal handed another one back, scratching at his bearded chin.

"One other thing—drop point's changed," Merei said. "Base of Comm Tower E-234. Same time."

The Gotal scowled. "In the middle of the grass-lands? Kriffing Laxo. What I am supposed to do, rent a tractor?"

"He said you wouldn't like it," Merei said.

"Which is why he did it," the Gotal said, scratching under one arm. "Tell that sleemo one day I'll drown him in hair oil—and it'll be the cut-rate stuff, not that imported glop he likes."

Merei hesitated, but she'd been told to expect something like that—and given a response to deliver.

"He said to tell you one day he'll put you in a pen with an electronic bell around your neck. One that plays the Imperial anthem every time you scratch a flea."

She braced herself for trouble, but the Gotal just whinnied in amusement and shook his head.

"Kriffing Laxo," he said as he shut the door. "See you next time, kid."

★ ★ ★

48

Merei visited Laxo's other three associates—a compulsive gambler who quaked in terror the moment she identified herself, a massive Herglic who smelled of fish and had a thick hide crisscrossed with scars, and a sardonic human in a mechno-chair who opened the door with a disruptor rifle in his lap. With her errands done, she raced across Capital City at an unsafe speed, arriving at V-SIS a few minutes before her first class.

She lifted her goggles and saw Jix Hekyl crossing the lawn. She wondered if he was returning from his own duties for the Gray Syndicate.

"Hey, Jix!" she called.

The Pantoran boy waited as Merei caught up to him.

"You weren't on the van," he said, looking puzzled.

"No," Merei said, brushing irritably at the dust covering her coat. "Jumpspeeder."

"So he's using you as a courier, then?"

"You should know better than to ask me that," Merei said.

Jix's cheeks darkened, and Merei smiled. But the smile faded away at the look of anguish on her fellow V-SIS student's face.

"I never should have gotten you involved with him," Jix said. "Now I worry about you all the time."

"I got myself involved with him," Merei said. "You

were just the guy who made the introductions. Anyway, it was worth it—lives were at stake."

"Yeah—like yours."

Jix hesitated, then leaned closer to her.

"Something went wrong, didn't it? With your snooper. You wouldn't be helping the Syndicate if it hadn't."

Merei looked out over the V-SIS lawn, which was turning yellow with the approach of winter. Beyond it she could see the towers of Capital City—a knot of white skyscrapers surrounding the mushroom-shaped Imperial headquarters.

Her first instinct was to tell Jix not to worry about it. It was her problem. But suddenly she found herself wanting to tell him—or perhaps it was just that she had to tell somebody. She couldn't tell Zare, not with the new Imperial security measures preventing them from speaking openly. And Zare had his own problems to deal with.

"Yes, something went wrong," she said. Then she told him about the broken chronometer on the computer at the Transportation Ministry, and how the Empire had found the snooper program and was now pursuing her.

Jix went pale.

"That's . . . that's pretty heavy weather. How do you know all that?"

"Well . . . my mother's the head of the anti-intrusion team investigating the break-in."

"You're kidding."

"Afraid not," she said, then told him about Jessa's investigation.

It turned out Jix could go even paler.

"Wow. Just . . . wow," he said. "And so Laxo's helping you?"

Merei shook her head. "Blackmailing me, you mean."

"He must like you."

"Lucky me."

"Yeah, really. So you've got two things to worry about—the witness who talked to you at the Transportation Ministry and whether they can recover your account from the repeater service. Which one did you use, if I can ask?"

"Bakiska's."

"Ooh. That's pretty basic. Laxo taught me how to bounce an encrypted request through multiple repeaters—that'll cover your tracks a lot better."

"Thanks. So do you know a way to erase my account at Bakiska's? Like, permanently erase it?"

Jix shook his head immediately.

"You can't do it remotely," he said. "You'd have to get access to the actual machine where that information's warehoused. Laxo's the same way—he won't back up any of his information, because he's afraid of remote intrusion. He keeps it all on that fancy network terminal behind his desk." Jix rolled his eyes. "Anyway, I know Bakiska's—their data center's on Lower Gallo. But they've got tough on-site security."

"You mean like data safeguards?" Merei asked.

"I mean like big, mean guys with guns."

Merei blew out her breath in frustration.

"Hey, one thing at a time," Jix said. "Let's start by making it impossible for that witness to identify you."

Merei looked at him in surprise.

"You mean . . ."

"What? Oh! No, no, nothing like that. I'll slice networks for Laxo, but nothing more than that. That's not what you meant, was it?"

"Of course not," Merei said, reddening.

They smiled at each other, embarrassed.

"What I meant was I can substitute someone else's picture for yours in the V-SIS records. If we pick one from some other school in Capital City, who's going to remember seeing the same person hundreds of pictures apart?"

"That'll work?" Merei asked.

"Probably," Jix said. "Particularly if, like your mother said, that witness isn't the brightest star in the sky."

"But isn't the V-SIS network hard to crack? This is a training ground for network-security specialists, after all. You'd think they'd have that data walled off."

Jix grinned.

"You'd think, but you'd be wrong. Grades and sensitive personal information are locked up pretty tight—tighter than the Imperial network, apparently—but stuff like images is pretty basic for a slicer with my skills."

"With your skills?" Merei asked teasingly.

"Yup," Jix said, now not shy at all. "We can get it done right now, in fact. Unless you have class."

"I can be late," Merei said. "Are you sure, Jix? I don't want to put you in danger, too."

"I helped get you into this mess. Please let me help get you out of it."

They made their way to the lowermost level and found an empty networking lab. Merei watched as Jix encrypted his machine's requests, logged on to a succession of repeater services, navigated to a data subnode, and then started working on finding an administrator account that he could slice.

"While I'm doing this, check the home data nodes for schools in Capital City," Jix said. "Find your replacement Merei Spanjaf—someone who looks a little like you, but not too close."

"Got it," Merei said, hunting through the public records of various schools. She listened to the clatter of Jix's fingers on his keyboard and sneaked a glance in the young slicer's direction. He was all business now, eyes fixed on the screen.

"I'm in," Jix said, grinning.

"That was fast," Merei said, and Jix shrugged with pretend modesty.

"So who's the new Merei?" he asked.

"Hestia Tarleton, of the Young Ladies' Seminary of Lothal Settlers. I'll comm you her picture."

"Got it," Jix said, peering at his screen. "Yeah, she looks like you. Though not as pretty."

Merei looked away, her face hot. After an awkward moment of silence, Jix started typing again.

"And . . . done," Jix said. "Now we've bought you some time."

He smiled shyly at her, and Merei found herself smiling back.

When Zare's turn for questioning finally came, he was momentarily worried that he would be sent to one of the interrogation rooms in Imperial headquarters. But instead he found himself in a featureless cubicle identical to the one where Currahee had interviewed him after his arrival at the Academy. Zare sat down at the bare metal table and waited.

After a few minutes, the door retracted into the wall and Lieutenant Chiron entered the little room, scowling down at the datapad in his hand.

"Cadet Leonis," he said, then shook his head. "What a nuisance to have to waste valuable training time on political nonsense. Particularly in your case—you just won a commendation, after all."

"We all have to do our duty, sir," Zare said, hoping his face hadn't betrayed his relief at seeing Chiron enter the room.

"Indeed we do. Well, at least the questionnaire is pretty standard. What do you say we get this over with, Zare?"

"Ready when you are, sir."

"Cadet Leonis, since arriving at the Academy, have you engaged in any act of treason against the Empire, aided such an act by someone else, or witnessed such an act and failed to report it to the proper authorities?"

Let's see, Zare thought. *I helped steal a decoder that was used by people dedicated to the Empire's overthrow. I stole an AT-DP pilot's blaster rifle and gave it to someone who used it to stun the pilot and a fellow cadet. I opened fire on an AT-DP, a troop transport, and numerous stormtroopers. I intentionally missed while firing at escaping enemies of the Empire. . . .*

"No, sir," he said.

Chiron made a note on his datapad.

"And before you arrived at the Academy, did you engage in any act of treason against the Empire, assist such an act by someone else, or witness such an act and fail to report it to the proper authorities?"

Would throwing a detonator at a troop transport count? I'm going to guess it would.

"No, sir," Zare said.

"Excellent," Chiron said, smiling. "Almost done with this charade, Zare."

Zare smiled back, but then looked down at the table. Chiron had always been good to him and was obviously convinced that Zare was the model cadet he'd tried to appear to be—just as Chiron was convinced that the Empire he served was a force for justice in the galaxy. The man was wrong on both counts, but he really believed he was doing the right thing.

"And are you currently planning to engage—" Chiron stopped as the door slid open behind him.

Captain Roddance entered the room, hands behind his back.

"I'll take it from here, Lieutenant," he said.

"There's no need, sir," Chiron said. "We were on the last question."

"I said I'll take it from here," Roddance repeated, his eyes growing cold and hard in his pale face.

"Of course, sir," Chiron said. He threw Zare a look that was equal parts puzzled and apologetic, and departed.

Roddance eyed the chair Chiron had abandoned, then pushed it in with one booted toe. He studied Zare for a moment, then took a datapad from behind his back.

"Let's dispense with this nonsense, cadet," Roddance said, placing the datapad on the table.

"Fine with me, sir," Zare said.

"Cadet Leonis, serious accusations have been made against you—ones that call into question your fitness for Imperial service."

Zare waited for the world to come tumbling down, wondering what name would indicate he was doomed. Had Beck finally been broken by the Empire's interrogators and confessed all? Or perhaps—and here Zare felt cold all over—Merei's slicing on his behalf had been discovered and she'd been hauled out of school by stormtroopers.

"Do you have any idea what these accusations might be, Cadet Leonis?" Roddance asked.

"No idea, sir."

"I see. You assaulted one of your instructors while a student at AppSci. Do you deny this?"

Of course! Fhurek! Zare scowled at the thought of the xenophobic athletic director who'd tried to keep him out of the Academy.

"No, sir," he said. "That's true."

"It is? Is an unprovoked attack on an instructor normal behavior for AppSci students, then? Surely you'd never think of attacking a superior officer here, Cadet Leonis."

"Of course not, sir. But the attack wasn't unprovoked, sir."

"Is that the case?"

"Athletic Director Fhurek suggested my sister was a traitor, sir. I'm not the least bit sorry for what I did."

Roddance raised an eyebrow.

"Cadet Dhara Leonis—your sister—deserted her squadmates, did she not?"

Zare swallowed hard. His hands were shaking. He thrust them under his legs and looked Roddance in the eye.

"No one knows what happened, sir," he said tightly. "But Dhara was Commandant Aresko's top cadet. She'd dreamed of serving the Empire all her life."

"So she said," Roddance said. "Did you know your sister was going to desert, Cadet Leonis?"

"Excuse me, sir?"

Roddance slammed his hand down on the table. Zare jumped, adrenaline shooting through him.

"Did you know your sister was going to desert? Answer the question, cadet!"

Roddance had both hands on the table and was leaning over it, staring at Zare.

"No," Zare said. "Of course not, sir."

"Did she ever express doubts about the Empire?"

"No."

"And your father? Did he ever question Imperial policies?"

"Only to argue they weren't tough enough," Zare said.

"Yes or no will do, cadet."

"That would be no, then," Zare said, folding his arms over his chest. "Sir."

"And your mother?"

"No, sir."

"And you? Have you ever expressed doubts about the Empire?"

"No, sir. Never."

"Then why, Cadet Leonis, did you withdraw your

application for this academy? Surely that indicates you had some kind of doubt about serving the Empire."

"My family was devastated by Dhara's disappearance, sir," Zare said. "And the Empire couldn't give us an answer about what happened. I couldn't bear the idea of putting my mom and dad through something like that again."

"And yet you reapplied," Roddance growled. "Why?"

"To restore my family's good name," Zare said, then stared hard at Roddance. "Which I've done during my time here."

"Ah, yes—you attempted to stop Morgan and Kell. Though that attempt was a failure."

"I did my best, sir."

"So you say, cadet. Did you know Morgan was going to do what he did?"

"Of course not, sir."

"And his collaborator? When did you know Jai Kell was planning to betray the Empire?"

"When he grabbed the pilot's blaster, sir."

"Of course," Roddance said. "What happened aboard that walker, Cadet Leonis?"

Zare leaned forward and put his elbows on the table, steepling his fingers.

"Exactly what I said in the report, sir."

"And what about Beck Ollet?"

"W-what?" Zare stammered.

"You heard me, cadet," Roddance growled. "Your AppSci teammate Beck Ollet. Your *friend* Beck Ollet. When was the last time you spoke to him?"

"This summer, sir," Zare said, trying to keep his hands still. "Before he set off on a jumpspeeder trip around Lothal. Before we got the news about what he'd done."

"The news that your friend attempted to murder Imperial personnel while they were carrying out their duties? Do you mean that news, Cadet Leonis?"

Zare thought back to the Westhills, to Roddance giving the order to round up the farmers who'd gathered to peacefully protest the confiscation and ruin of properties that had been in their families for generations. He remembered how the stormtroopers had waded into the crowd, stunning some people and beating others with their rifles. How Zare and Beck had heard the crack of blaster fire and known it meant people were dying.

"Yes, sir," he said quietly. "I mean that news."

"And did you know Ollet was planning such an attack?"

"Of course not, sir," Zare said.

"Of course not," Roddance said with a sneer. "And

did your good friend Beck Ollet ever express political opinions?"

"Political opinions?" Zare asked, thinking desperately about what the Empire must already know, what Beck would have told them under interrogation. "He was upset about his family's orchards being turned into a location for mining."

"And did you report his remarks to that effect, Cadet Leonis?"

"No, sir."

"Why didn't you? Do I need to explain to you that your carelessness led to the loss of innocent lives? Or that it is the duty of all Imperial citizens to report suspicious activity to the authorities?"

"Beck had a right to be upset," Zare said. "But I never thought he'd do anything like that."

"The right to be upset? On what grounds?"

"P-progress means change, sir," Zare stammered. "And change can be hard for some people to accept."

He sounded like his father on one of his worse days, Zare thought dismally. Or like some junior version of Alton Kastle. Or like any of a million other Imperials who acted as accessories to cruelty and murder.

"It's all very convenient, Cadet Leonis," Roddance hissed. "You have so many connections to people who have engaged in seditious acts against Imperial authority, yet somehow none of those people can be questioned. Your sister is missing. Morgan and Kell are fugitives. And Beck Ollet is unavailable for questioning."

Roddance leaned forward, his gloved fingertip a centimeter from Zare's face.

"Given your history of suspicious associations, Leonis, I recommended that you be turned over to the Imperial Security Bureau for interrogation," he said.

Zare swallowed hard. He'd heard tales of torture droids and screams that made even hardened soldiers stand a little farther from detention cells.

"That request was denied," Roddance said. "It seems you have friends in high places. But know this, Leonis— I'm not one of them. I'll be watching you."

Zare leaned back, away from that accusatory finger.

"I have done my duty, sir," he said stiffly. "I have nothing to be ashamed of."

Roddance nodded, then pulled out the chair on the other side of the table and sat down. He was calm now—so calm that Zare wondered how much of the questioning had been an act.

"You've been selected for one final exercise, Cadet Leonis," Roddance said, thumbing his comlink. "I don't claim to understand its purpose, but the request also came from the highest levels."

Roddance glanced at Zare, whose look of puzzlement

was entirely genuine. The door opened, and a junior officer handed Roddance a curious device—a screen with a handle on it.

Zare wondered if the device was some kind of old-fashioned datapad. Then Roddance turned it around so Zare could see the screen. The simplified image of a starship appeared, followed by a cup and then a speeder.

Roddance turned the device around again so Zare could see nothing but its featureless back.

"A ship, a cup, a speeder," Roddance said. "Now, Cadet Leonis. Tell me what's on the screen."

PART 2:
JUSTICE

For a few days Merei was too frightened to ask her mother for an update about the investigation into the break-in at the Transportation Ministry. But then Jessa brought it up herself one morning, just as Gandr was setting poached eggs on the table.

"At the risk of sounding disloyal, the Transportation Ministry would be better off if it hired blind Tavelian cavefish," she muttered. "We've shown every witness who spoke to the girl selling raffle tickets the image of every teenage girl who attends school within five hundred kilometers of Capital City. And none of them has recognized her. I'm starting to think she was a ghost."

"So maybe your intruder wasn't a schoolgirl," Merei said, trying not to betray her relief with a smile. Jix's image switcheroo had worked.

"I thought of that," Jessa said. "We know every farm girl being taught at home, and every religious and cultural exception granted by the Education Ministry. We have images of all of those girls. There's no match. And there's no match in any law-enforcement database."

"So she isn't from Lothal," Gandr said.

"Possibly," Jessa said. "In which case there's no point showing images at all. Include Lothal's neighbors within just twenty light-years and you're talking about millions of pictures. We'd be sitting there until the sun went dark."

"So are they closing the case?" Merei dared to ask. "I mean, you've never said anything valuable was accessed."

"Because we don't know that," Jessa said. "No, the case is still very much open. This just means we can't do it the easy way. The next step is to give the intrusion pattern to the repeater services on Lothal and demand that they look for a match. Once we get a match, we get a warrant for any records for the account. And then we'll have the origin point of whoever accessed the snooper's data."

Merei tried to imagine her mother's face when she saw that the origin point was her own house. But of course she'd never see that moment. Merei's only indication that it had happened would be a knock at the door and a demand to open up.

"And how long will that take?" Merei asked her mother.

Jessa warmed her hands on her teacup, lips pursed as she considered the question.

"Well, we've caught a break there," she said. "Given recent events—such as the terrorist attack on Empire Day—the courts are granting security-related requests with a lot less fuss than they used to. The repeater services will fight a warrant, but they'll lose. Then it depends on what kind of pattern we have and how many access records might be a match."

"So how long?" Merei forced herself to ask again, trying to wet her lips with a suddenly dry tongue.

"I'd guess a few weeks maybe," Jessa said, then smiled. "At most."

Rosey didn't like having to transport Merei's jump-speeder in the back of the speeder van with them, but Laxo had insisted. So Merei's mornings were spent holding the speeder steady against the threat of potholes while Laxo's thugs complained.

"I'm gonna ask the boss to let me deliver messages," said the mustachioed human thug named Ort. "I'm a lot scarier than this pipsqueak girl."

He leaned forward and ran his hands covetously over Merei's jumpspeeder, showing his yellow teeth in a feral grin.

"Besides, I already got me a jumpspeeder," he said. "Or at least I'd have one after I'd wrung a certain brat's skinny neck."

Merei had had enough.

"Hey, Ort, you ever think about why your duties are limited to riding around in the back of this van?" she asked. "It's because you couldn't wring my neck if you had written instructions. Teaching you to read an address would be like training a Loth-rat to fly a TIE fighter."

While Ort was working this through, the other thug—his name was Gort or Vort or something—started to laugh. Apparently, he hadn't reached the conclusion that his duties were no more complicated than Ort's.

Rosey looked away in disgust, shaking her head.

Merei could tell Ort had finished his mental gymnastics because he started fumbling for his blaster.

"Why, you little—" he growled. But his hands froze as Rosey drew her own blaster and pointed it at his head.

"Uh-uh, Ort," the Rodian warned. "You had that coming. From now on, when this one's around, you keep your mouth shut."

Ort subsided with a last poisonous glower at Merei. Rosey turned to Merei, wagging one finger in warning.

"As for you, watch your mouth," she said. "You know the difference between the boss and me? It's that he likes you."

"Sorry, Rosey," Merei said sweetly. She leaned back against the swaying side of the van, fighting the urge to smile.

Guess I'm moving up in the world, she thought.

When they got to Laxo's headquarters, one of his thugs looked up from playing sabacc and said the crime boss wanted to see her. Merei exchanged a puzzled glance with Jix, then climbed the stairs. Rosey followed right behind her.

She wondered if she'd gone too far by provoking Ort. But there was no way Laxo had received a message from Rosey since the incident in the van, let alone from Ort or Gort/Vort. Merei seriously doubted the two humans could type, anyway.

"New procedure, kid," Laxo said with a grin, propping his lilac slippers up on his fancy desk. "I'm giving you the address of this place so we don't waste time ferrying you back and forth. You have to memorize it—don't write it down, and don't ever enter it into your datapad. Can you do that?"

"I don't need to," Merei said. "The address here is 5025 Edgemoor."

Laxo looked accusingly at Rosey, who shrugged. Her bumpy skin had gone pale green with fear.

"I didn't say anything, boss!"

"Don't blame Rosey," Merei said. "Your driver takes the exact same turns every morning. I memorized them, then traced them on a map."

Rosey and Laxo exchanged a glance. Then the crime boss brayed with laughter.

"This is why I don't let Rosey shoot you, kid," Laxo said. "You're smart and you don't scare."

Merei supposed it was good that Laxo had no idea how frightened she was every day—that what he saw as fearlessness was really a hopeless show of defiance. She was going to be caught and sent to prison, or worse, and if there was no chance of escaping it, there was also no reason to take a lot of garbage from a bunch of two-credit Old City thugs.

"I want you on the road earlier because I've got a new job for you," Laxo said.

"Not running pirated grav-ball holos out to Old Jho again," Merei pleaded. "That place is the back of beyond."

"Not this time. It's another one of my little business ventures—hiding people."

"Hiding people from whom?"

"Oh, that depends," Laxo said, reshaping his pompadour with a few languid pats. "People around here have so many things to hide from. Business associates who feel wronged. Jealous romantic partners with hot tempers. And of course the long arm of Imperial justice."

"You hide people from the Empire?" Merei asked.

"Of course I do," Laxo said, then rubbed the fingers of one hand together. "Got a few stashed away right now—there's Holshef, Pinson, and a couple of others. I hide them as long as they've got enough credits, you understand."

"I figured as much," Merei said.

Laxo grinned. She noticed that he had beautiful teeth.

"Clever girl," he said with a yawn.

A moment after Zare commed Merei, he wished he hadn't: she had deep bags under her eyes, and her hand shook as she reached for her datapad's screen. Zare pressed his own hand to the cam unit on his side, then stared helplessly at her.

"I rode past the Academy this morning," Merei said. "I waved to you. Even though I knew you couldn't see me. Isn't that stupid?"

"I wish I'd known—I would have waved back. What time was this?"

"About 0600 I think."

"Oh. I wasn't there. We were running in the Easthills. It was only ten klicks, though. Curry was feeling merciful."

"So I waved to you and you weren't even there," Merei said.

She blinked furiously, turning away from the camera.

"Hey," Zare said. "I'm glad you did. Why were you up so early?"

"Oh, doing things before school. Errands."

"At 0600? You must have been in the marketplace, then. That's the only place I can think of that's open that early."

"Yeah," Merei said after a moment. "I was in the marketplace."

Zare nodded, not sure what to say. It was obvious Merei was upset. But was she in danger? He couldn't tell—and all of a sudden that was unbearable to him. He wanted to demand that she tell him what was wrong so he could comfort her, reassure her, like he was supposed to.

I will, he thought. *The Empire can't monitor everything. Odds are no one will ever know.*

He opened his mouth, then shut it again. Roddance had warned him that he would be watching—which meant he was probably listening, as well.

Zare shook his head sadly instead.

"So how are the drills going?" Merei asked.

"Oh, you know, they're drills," Zare said, then hesitated.

If the Empire's agents are listening, it means they aren't noting just what I say, he thought. *They'll also be paying attention to what I* don't *say—and wondering why I would leave something out.*

"There was this one strange drill I didn't understand," Zare said. "They showed me pictures of stuff on a little screen, like a datapad. A ship. Then a cup. Then a speeder. Then they turned the screen around and asked me to tell them what was on it."

He stared into the camera, hoping Merei saw the warning in his eyes.

She leaned back, blinking, and Zare could see her

mind working. He smiled. She was never more beautiful than when she was breaking down a problem.

If I had the Force, maybe I could hug her right through the camera.

"That is strange," Merei said. "How did you do?"

"I don't know. And no one's said when I'll find out."

Merei nodded. Zare could see the alarm in her face, in the way her mouth was set in a grim line and her eyes were fixed straight ahead.

"Well," she said, forcing a smile onto her face. "I hope you passed."

"Maybe I'll know by winter break. It's not so far off, you know."

"You keep saying that," Merei said with a sigh.

"I know. But it's actually true."

Merei woke up in the middle of the night and couldn't go back to sleep. First she was thinking of Zare, of him sitting in the Academy guessing at pictures on a screen. She knew the test had to do with the mysterious Force he'd told her about, the power some people could use to see things that were far away and move objects with their minds.

Zare had told her about the gamble he'd taken with the Imperial agent he called the Inquisitor, how he'd tried to fool the being into thinking he shared his sister's abilities with the Force. As far as Zare knew, he had no such talents—and Merei had never seen any signs of them, either.

If the Empire's tests had shown that Zare couldn't use the Force, what would it mean? Would this Inquisitor conclude that Zare was lying and come to take him away? If that happened, she'd never know. Zare would simply disappear, as Dhara had.

But what if the tests had shown that Zare *was* Force-sensitive? What if he had some ability that had gone undetected? Wouldn't that bring the Inquisitor, too?

And which scenario was worse?

Merei stared at the ceiling. It was awful not being able to talk with him, to have to speak in useless code. He had no idea the danger she was in—that she was trying to escape her own mother and avoid being drawn deeper into Laxo's web. She hadn't told Zare because she hadn't wanted to add to his burdens, and now she *couldn't* tell him.

She couldn't tell him about bringing messages to Laxo's clients and underlings, about trying to look tough when confronted by thugs and gamblers. Nor could she tell him about her latest job for the Gray Syndicate— collecting credits from fugitives who were paying Laxo to hide them, and telling them when they'd be moved to one of the other hidey-holes he kept in Capital City.

She couldn't tell him about Holshef, for instance.

Most of Laxo's fugitives were lowlifes ducking gambling debts or other self-inflicted trouble. But Holshef was different. He'd looked delighted to see her, inviting her into his hidden warren on the lowest level of an Old City warehouse and offering her a cup of tarine tea.

Holshef was a tiny old man, pale in a way that made her fear for his health, with a halo of wispy white hair. He gave her Laxo's credits, then asked her about the weather, what color the grass was, and if the dust storms were turning the sunsets a deeper orange and purple.

He was terribly lonely, she realized—lonely, with a deep sadness about him.

Merei had told him about how the grass was yellowing, and that the Weather Ministry didn't think the dust storms would be anything extraordinary this year but that every week seemed to prove them wrong. Then she'd asked if she could ask *him* something.

Holshef had nodded, and she'd apologetically asked what he was hiding from. He didn't seem like a gambler or a smuggler on the lam. What had he done?

"I wrote poetry," he said. "And painted."

"Are those crimes?" Merei had asked.

"They are if they're about what's being lost on Lothal," Holshef had replied. "I was happy when the Empire annexed the planet—we threw a party! I even invited my most boring cousins. There's so much the Empire could do to bind the galaxy together, to create a more perfect union of worlds the way the Republic never could. But what has it done instead? Poisoned Lothal's air and water, when protecting them would have only cost a few percentage points of profit. I thought that was wrong, and I thought surely someone in the Empire would understand it was wrong. I thought if I pointed it out, someone would stop it."

Merei had nodded grimly. She'd thought the same thing once, and she'd even tried to persuade Beck Ollet that was the case. But she'd been wrong, and Beck had been right. He'd fought for those beliefs and disappeared.

"So I wrote poems," Holshef had concluded. "And I painted. I don't see why that should be a crime—or why there should be a warrant for my arrest. I keep thinking I should end this charade and go see Governor Pryce. She'll understand."

"No, she won't," Merei had said.

"That's what my daughter says, too. So it's hide here in the dark instead."

Then Holshef had smiled and patted her hand.

"But it's nice to see a friendly face," he said. "I'll paint you a picture—don't worry, it won't be anything that might get you in trouble, too. Please tell me you'll come back."

Merei jammed her pillow over her face, trying to force herself to go back to sleep. She'd be back as long as Holshef's credits held out—or Laxo didn't change his mind. Neither struck her as much of a guarantee of the old poet's safety.

What have I gotten myself into? She wondered, not for the first time. *And how do I get myself out of it?*

When Merei arrived the next morning, Jix was waiting in Laxo's office, looking frightened.

"There you are, kiddo," Laxo said. "Before you start your rounds, I need you to take this one over to a client's shop—I'm renting him out for a special slicing job. Rosey tells me young Jixy here always seems to work a little harder when you're around, so I figure this is a good way to motivate him."

Merei knew without even looking at him that Jix would be blushing—and she realized she was blushing, too.

Laxo laughed.

"Young love," he said. "It gladdens the heart. Oh, wait a sec, kid—it's payday."

Merei looked at Laxo in surprise, wondering if that was code for some new duty. But Laxo handed her a small satchel of credit chips. She looked in the bag and was stunned to find nearly a thousand credits inside.

"I may not be a traditional employer, but I treat my people well," Laxo said. "Remember that when I'm running the entire underworld here on Lothal."

"What do the real crime bosses think of you bragging like that?" Merei asked.

She heard Jix stifle a gasp behind her. But Laxo just chuckled.

"Right now they barely think of me at all—which is exactly how I like it. But give it time, kids. Give it time. Now get going—it's time to get to work."

Merei tucked the bag full of credits in her carryall and tramped down the stairs, Jix hurrying after her. She got on the jumpspeeder and fired up the engine, then looked up to find Jix standing uncertainly on the curb.

"Well, come on," she said. "Get on behind me."

"Um, okay," Jix said.

She felt his weight settle onto the jumpspeeder.

"I recommend holding on," Merei said after a moment. "Around my waist."

Jix put his arms around her waist, and Merei could feel his breath on her neck. His arms felt nice, she realized.

She shook the thought away. *You have a boyfriend. Remember?*

Currahee gave the order for dismissal, and the Academy's cadets broke ranks with a cheer, hurrying across the plaza to their waiting parents and siblings. Zare kept his cool until his mother enfolded him in her arms and he felt her tears on the back of his neck. When Tepha Leonis finally let go, he was wiping at his own eyes.

"Now, Tepha—don't smother the boy," said Leo Leonis with a smile. He shook his son's hand, then drew Zare into another embrace, his hands thumping Zare's back.

"I swear you've grown two or three centimeters," Tepha said, her hand on Zare's face. "Don't you think so, Merei?"

"At least that," Merei said, and then she was pulling Zare to her. She closed her eyes and let out a ragged breath.

"I've missed you so much," she said. "You can't even imagine."

"Let's go," Tepha said. "Auntie Nags has prepared a feast. Are you sure you can't come, Merei?"

"I'm sure," Merei said apologetically. "I have exams tomorrow—I could only sneak away for a minute. But I'll be over right after exams are done, okay?"

"All right then," Tepha said. "Two feasts. Can we give you a lift at least?"

"I've got my jumpspeeder," Merei said. She turned to go, then stopped to pull Zare close again. When they drew apart, her cheeks were wet.

"Hey," Zare said. "We made it."

"I keep telling myself that," Merei said.

Zare woke up with a start and looked at the clock. It read 0545—but of course there was no Currahee shouting for worthless cadets to get out of their bunks, threatening demerits and extra kitchen duty. He blew his breath out and rolled over, stuffing his head under the pillow. But sleep wouldn't come. The bed felt too soft, like he was in danger of being swallowed by it, and he kept thinking that he'd missed reveille and would get written up.

He gave up and padded into the kitchen, where Auntie Nags was puttering about. The old nanny droid never slept, unless her rare maintenance cycles counted as sleep. She heard him and turned, photoreceptors turning green.

"Zare Leonis! You're up early! How about a mug of hot chocolate?"

That sounded wonderful, and Zare sat savoring the warm drink at the kitchen table while Nags fussed over him, chattering about how empty the apartment had seemed. Without him and without . . . and then she stopped, photoreceptors flaring yellow.

"Oh my," she said. "My apologies, Zare. How thoughtless of me."

"It's okay, Nags," Zare said. "I miss her, too. Every day."

"She'd be so proud of you. When she was home a year ago, she talked about how she couldn't wait for you to learn everything she was learning. She was sitting right where you are now."

Zare accepted another mug of hot chocolate, but his parents heard Nags talking to him and got out of bed. Within a few minutes, Alton Kastle was delivering the news while Leo insisted that the Empire needed to crack down on the current plague of lawlessness.

"The attack at the Academy, and now Empire Day. No one will say it, but these are not just isolated incidents," Leo said. "There's a pattern behind it—something dangerous. Dangerous to commerce, and authority, and the social order."

Zare looked miserably at his mother, who knew what his father didn't—that Alton Kastle was an Imperial stooge and much of the news he delivered was either carefully manicured truth or entirely fictitious.

"Oh, Leo, let's not ruin a nice morning," she said. "I hope Merei does well on her exams."

Leo either hadn't heard his wife or was ignoring her.

"At least Governor Pryce is still on top of things," he said. "Her assistant assures me that her office is doing everything it can to find your sister, Zare. I'm certain it's one of her highest priorities."

"I hope so, Dad," Zare said, his anger with his father now mixed with pity. "What are we doing today, anyway?"

"Why, nothing, dear," Tepha said. "We thought you'd want a day without being told what to do every single minute."

Zare nodded. "That sounds great."

But it wasn't great—not at all. He felt adrift all of a sudden. There was no schedule to tell him how to fill up all the hours ahead of him. He went into his bedroom and started to flop down on the bed, but he'd made it and couldn't stand the idea of messing up the precise line of the sheet and the neat, wrinkle-free cover. He stood staring down at it for nearly a minute, then sat at his desk and stared out the window at the grasslands, turned a pale pink by the rising sun.

Dhara had experienced this, too, he remembered, on

her own winter break a year ago. She'd laughed at his look of horror when he saw her perfectly made bed, and at his insistence that he'd never do such a thing unless forced. She'd known what lay ahead for him, what Academy life would do to him.

She'd known that, but she'd had no way of knowing what lay ahead for herself.

He stared out the window as the sun crept up the vault of the sky. At the Academy he'd had something to do, at least. At home there was nothing to do but wonder if that was the day his sister would die—while he sat there doing nothing.

Merei had said she'd come over right after exams, and Zare ran downstairs the moment she commed him to say she was a block away. He hugged her, his head wreathed in his own breath.

She hugged him back, but then looked at what he was wearing and frowned. "A T-shirt and shorts? You must be freezing!"

"I really want to go for a run," he explained. "I figured we could talk while we're doing that. Are you up for it?"

"Run? And talk at the same time? No, I'm not up for that. That sounds awful, in fact."

"Oh," Zare said, looking crestfallen.

Merei shook her head, smiling.

"How about you run and I keep pace on my speeder? I think I can handle that and a conversation at the same time."

Zare nodded and set off with Merei idling alongside him, the jumpspeeder's engine purring beneath her.

"It's such a relief to get to talk to you," Zare said as they reached the other side of the marketplace. "I thought I was going to go crazy when we couldn't do that."

"Me too," Merei said. "Except you aren't talking to me."

"I'm sorry. It's just . . . I don't know where to start."

"Really? Zare, it's me. It doesn't matter where you start. Talk to me. Please?"

Zare nodded, breathing hard now, and started telling her about Oleg, and Roddance, and how he'd been questioned. They left the city behind and started to climb into the Easthills, with Zare running faster and faster, until he was flying along the roadway and Merei had to yell over her jumpspeeder's engine.

"Zare, stop," she said, hitting the brake. The jumpspeeder halted, but Zare kept running, only turning around when he realized she was no longer beside him.

"What's wrong?" he asked, hands on his knees.

"*You're* what's wrong," Merei said. "You're killing yourself. Are you planning to run all the way to Coruscant?"

Zare looked puzzled.

"We do this every morning. I don't know—it's a relief somehow."

"Is this the same route you run at the Academy?" Merei asked.

"Yes. Just a little farther?"

Zare began to run again. Merei shook her head and drove after him, and he kept talking. He told her about exercises and drills, and at first she was sympathetic: he clearly needed to let go of everything he'd been bottling up inside. But then her sympathy began to ebb. He hadn't asked her anything about her own situation beyond a few questions about exams.

"Zare," she said when she could no longer take it. "Don't you want to know what's happening in *my* life?"

He heard the anger in her voice and stopped running. That was something, at least.

"I'm sorry," he said. "Of course I do."

And so she told him—and watched his concern turn to alarm, and then explode into panic.

"You never told me any of this," he said, and she

drew back instinctively. It sounded like he was accusing her.

"I didn't want to right after the Inquisitor, and Dev and Jai," she said. "And then I couldn't until now."

"I thought you said you'd gotten away with it," he said, his voice rising. "That your snooper things had left no trace that anyone could follow."

"That's what I thought, too. I was wrong."

"You have to stop, Merei," he said, his eyes wide and frantic. "Stop dealing with this Laxo person. Stop and . . . and . . ."

"And what, Zare? You tell me what I should do. Tell my mother? Turn myself in to the Empire? I can't stop, Zare. I haven't figured out what to do yet, but I do know that stopping isn't an option. You understand that, don't you?"

Zare shook his head. He put his hand to his face, then thrust it out in front of him, like he was trying to keep something dangerous at bay.

"I—I can't do this," he said. "I thought you were safe, Merei. You told me you were safe! I'll lose my mind if I have to worry about you and Dhara at the same time!"

"You'll lose *your* mind? I'm sorry to add to your burdens! I'm sorry that my impending arrest and trial for treason is making your life harder!"

Zare was staring at her. The wind had picked up and was whistling through the grasslands. Merei pulled her jacket tighter around her.

"Merei, I'm sorry," Zare said, looking stricken. "I . . . I didn't think. It's all been too much, and I . . . I didn't think."

She shut off the speeder and got off it, her legs shaky.

"Come here," she said. "Please."

"I'm disgusting," Zare said. "Soaked with sweat."

She looked at him, and he spread his arms helplessly.

"I will later," he promised.

The wind whistled past them. Merei blinked away the ever-present dust.

"We should go back," Merei said.

She started up her jumpspeeder. Zare began to walk, and Merei kept her speeder at a walking pace next to him, neither of them saying anything.

It wasn't until the last day of break that Zare got a chance to talk with his mother alone for more than a few minutes.

Tepha suggested that Zare accompany her to the marketplace, which Leo detested as loud, crowded, and unruly. Zare knew what his mother was up to even before Tepha locked eyes with him across the kitchen, and he gamely volunteered that he'd like to get some snacks to bring back to the barracks. Then all they had to do was fend off Auntie Nags's insistence that she come and carry parcels.

"I'd hoped we'd see more of Merei while you were home," Tepha said. "But I understand she's busy with her studies."

Zare nodded. He couldn't talk about the fact that Merei was spending more and more time doing Laxo's business both before and after school, and he didn't want to talk about the fact that something had been lost between them. He'd seen her several times since their argument in the Easthills, but they'd avoided discussing the Academy or anything about Laxo—which meant they'd spent too much of their time together in silence.

"Zare, I'm worried," his mother said when they were a few blocks from the marketplace.

Part of him wanted to laugh. Another part of him wanted to ask her how worried she imagined he was, spending days and nights surrounded by enemies and waiting to disappear as his sister had.

Instead he forced himself to exhale. His mother knew the dangers, of course. And at least he had things to fill his day. All Tepha could do was mourn the child she'd lost and wonder if she'd lose the other.

"I'm worried, too, Mom," he said.

"I lie awake thinking of Dhara in that terrible place on Arkanis and, and . . ."

She stopped, one hand pressed to her mouth. Zare squeezed her shoulder.

"I know," he said. "I do, too. It makes me crazy to think how long it will take me to get there."

He almost added, *If I get there at all.* But he refused to entertain that thought. One way or another, he would get to Arkanis.

"But that's it, Zare," Tepha said. "What if you get to Arkanis and . . ."

"Disappear, too?"

Tepha nodded. "You know the Academy here on Lothal. But you don't know anything about that place. You don't know what's waiting for you there."

Zare looked around warily. Tepha saw it and her eyes widened.

"Is it as bad as that?"

"I don't know," Zare said. He doubted the Empire would spy on random pedestrians in Capital City. But then not so long ago, he would never have believed the Empire would monitor top ministers' communications within Imperial headquarters. And not so long before that, he would have been astonished and offended by the idea that the Empire would do anything that wasn't in the interests of its citizens.

"We've talked about this, Mom," Zare said. "We know she was taken to Arkanis. My only chance of finding her is to get there myself."

They were on the edge of the marketplace. Zare started to ask his mother which errand they should pursue first, then stopped. People were rushing toward them, looking nervously over their shoulders.

"Mom, wait," Zare said.

A squad of stormtroopers was marching through the marketplace, shoving a gangly, long-nosed Faust male in binders ahead of it. Two of the troopers stopped at a stall, and Zare could hear the buzz of their electronically modulated voices. A diminutive Ugnaught shrugged, and a moment later he was kneeling with an E-11 behind his head as another trooper slapped cuffs on him.

"What's happening?" asked Tepha.

"I don't know," Zare said. "But I think we'd better get home."

On the way back to the Leonises' apartment, they saw stormtroopers knocking on doors and manning vehicle checkpoints. Troop transports were out in the streets, cruising slowly as troopers stared at pedestrians and vehicles.

When they reached the apartment, Leo was sitting in front of the telecaster, smiling and nodding.

"There you are!" he said. "Come listen—Alton Kastle is speaking live from Imperial headquarters. They're finally doing it!"

"Doing what, Dad?" Zare asked. "What's happening?"

"A crackdown on dissent and sedition," Leo said. "It's planetwide, Governor Pryce says. Kallus from the Imperial Security Bureau is leading it, and the governor is pledging the support of all ministries. She said all military personnel will be involved."

"Oh dear," said Auntie Nags, photoreceptors flaring yellow.

"*All* military personnel?" Tepha asked. "That wouldn't include cadets, though. Would it, Zare?"

"It might," Leo said. He reached up and gave Zare a friendly punch on the shoulder. "Looks like you'll get a chance to prove your mettle, son. I know you'll make us proud."

The cadets returned from winter break and were summoned to the main hangar at dawn, where Captain Roddance awaited them, standing on a platform hovering two meters above the floor. He was wearing a helmet and body armor that covered his chest, shoulders, and arms.

"Never seen the Rodder wearing field armor before," Kabak whispered to Rykoff as their fellow cadets filed in behind them. Chiron and Currahee stood below the platform in their gray-green Imperial uniforms.

"Guess the crackdown's serious," Rykoff replied.

The two cadets had their faceplates up. Zare whispered at them to be quiet, but it was too late: Currahee quelled the surreptitious conversations in the ranks with a furious demand for silence, her face bright red.

"Welcome back, cadets," Roddance said, staring down at them. "There will be no training exercises today. Or for the foreseeable future."

A few cadets cheered and were swiftly silenced by squadmates who were quicker on the uptake. Currahee looked like she was ready to strangle someone.

"Rather than training, you will be in the field," Roddance said. "Your mission is to help ensure public safety and security by detecting illegal activity and eliminating it. Your performance at this academy will no longer be measured by how you do during training exercises, but by how many violations of Imperial law you help uncover."

The cadets shifted uncertainly, trying to make sense of these new orders.

"You'll work in pairs, with each of you receiving a comlink, binders, and a stun rifle," Roddance said. "Lieutenant Chiron and Sergeant Currahee will assign each pair to a grid of city blocks. You'll go door-to-door, making sure all residents are registered with the Empire and asking them about illegal activities they've observed. If you observe criminal activity firsthand or if any citizen refuses to comply with this lawful order, you may either take them into custody or contact one of the stormtrooper units that will be supporting you."

Zare swallowed hard. As a child he'd imagined himself wearing the uniform of the Empire and bringing its enemies to justice. But in his fantasies, those enemies had been pirates, slavers, or Separatist holdouts—not ordinary citizens who could be arrested for refusing to inform on their neighbors.

"You may encounter citizens who question the need for this action or object to how it will be conducted," Roddance said. "This in itself is a violation of Imperial law—record it and report it. Remind everyone you speak to that Imperial law demands that any illegal act—no matter how small—be reported. Vigilance is our duty, not a luxury."

Next to Zare, Oleg smiled broadly, clearly excited. Roddance caught Oleg's eye and gave him a nod.

"Ladies and gentlemen, playtime is over," he said. "Do I make myself clear, cadets?"

Zare's stomach twisted, and for a moment he feared he was going to throw up right in front of Roddance.

"Sir, yes, sir!" he bellowed along with the other cadets.

Roddance marched out of the hangar, passing glossy black work droids carrying equipment crates.

Currahee ordered Unit Aurek to step forward. Still feeling queasy, Zare clipped the comlink, binders, and datapad to his belt, then checked his blaster's power levels and slid it into his holster.

"Unit Aurek, you have been assigned grids 17A and B," Chiron said. "You'll see the outlines of your search area on your helmets' heads-up displays. Two of you will take 17A, the other two 17B."

Zare wondered if he'd be assigned Kabak or Rykoff as a partner. He hoped it would be Rykoff. He was a little calmer than Kabak, and emotions were likely to spill over during this mission.

"Cadets Kabak and Rykoff, you'll be working as one team," Chiron said.

Zare and Oleg looked at each other in surprise and dismay.

"That can't be right," Oleg said. "Someone's made a mistake."

"Wouldn't it make more sense to have a more experienced cadet on each team, sir?" asked Zare.

Chiron smiled thinly.

"After all this time, we've found something you two agree on," he said. "There's no mistake, cadets. Captain Roddance requested this pairing personally. Now double-check your gear and get ready to move out."

Zare nodded unhappily. Chiron's eyes held his for a long moment, and Zare could read the warning there.

The interior of the troop transport was dim and quiet; Zare sat with his elbows on his knees, trying not to think about how excited his younger self would have been to ride in such an Imperial war machine.

The transport glided to a halt, and a young Imperial officer turned and nodded at the two cadets. It was the first time he'd acknowledged them during the journey from the Academy.

"We have our own search grid a couple of blocks over. If you have any trouble, contact us immediately. Make sure you record each civilian encounter—if I have to search this grid again because a couple of kids messed up, I'll report it to Captain Roddance."

"We know our mission, sir," Zare said grimly.

"Good," the officer said as the rear hatch hissed open, leaving Zare and Oleg blinking away the bright light of morning. "Get to it, then."

"I'll take the lead in the questioning," Zare told Oleg.

Oleg narrowed his eyes. "Who put you in charge, Leonis?"

"Someone has to take the lead."

"We'll take turns, then."

Zare couldn't think of a reason to object to that and nodded unhappily.

"Me first, then you," Zare said, and Oleg shrugged. "And keep your faceplate raised."

"Why?"

"Because people are going to be frightened," Zare said. "If they can see our faces, they'll be more likely to relax and tell us what we need to know."

"You're wrong," Oleg said. "They won't respect us if they see we're kids. But they will respect the face of the Empire. Which is this."

He lowered his helmet's faceplate, leaving Zare looking at the skull-like mask.

"Do it your way, then," Zare said contemptuously, ringing the buzzer beside the door of a low-slung house whose small front yard was barren but free of litter.

"Yes?" a woman's voice asked timidly through the speaker grille.

"Imperial security sweep, ma'am," Zare said. "We have a few questions to ask you."

"I'm making breakfast," the woman said. "You'll have to come back later."

She clicked off. Zare looked at the speaker grille in consternation.

"Are you going to let her treat you like a door-to-door salesman?" Oleg asked with a sneer, reaching for the comm panel.

Zare smacked his hand away.

"It's still my turn, remember?"

He pressed down the call button again.

"Like I just told you—"

"Ma'am, I'm afraid you're required to answer our questions by order of the governor," Zare said. "It will only take a couple of minutes."

The line was silent for a moment, then the woman sighed and clicked off. A moment later the front door opened and a Sullustan woman glared at the two cadets, her big ears twitching with annoyance.

"What's so important, then? I'm very busy."

"I'm Cadet Leonis, and this is Cadet Oleg," Zare said. "Is everyone at this residence registered with the Empire?"

The Sullustan nodded, wiping flour from her hands with a towel.

"Do you know of any illegal activities in the area? I assure you, everything you tell us will be kept confidential, ma'am."

The Sullustan's dark eyes narrowed.

"Illegal activities? Such as what?"

Oleg stepped forward, but Zare held up his hand to silence him.

"Theft, blackmail, things like that," Zare said.

The woman shook her head.

"This is a quiet block," she said. "I don't know everything my neighbors do, but they seem like good enough people. Now is there anything else?"

"No, ma'am," Zare said. "Thank you for your time."

The door shut, and Zare filed the report on his datapad.

"Is that it?" Oleg sneered, his voice electronically modulated. "Are you finished being useless, Leonis?"

"That's it. Next house is yours."

"Good," Oleg said. "Now watch how a real cadet gets results."

He marched over to the next house and held down the call buzzer for a full five seconds.

"What is it?" a man asked, sounding both sleepy and annoyed.

"Imperial security sweep. You have sixty seconds to come outside."

"What? Hang on, hang on."

The man's face was puffy with sleep. He blinked quizzically at the two cadets standing in his front yard.

"Is everyone in this house registered with the Empire?" Oleg demanded.

"I am—I work on the line for Sienar Fleet Systems, so I was registered automatically. My wife and son haven't yet because—"

"Failure to register is a violation of Imperial law," Oleg said.

"We just didn't get to it yet," the man said. "My farming collective got sold to the Empire, which shut it down. I came to Capital City a month ago, and we've been working double shifts—"

"That's not an excuse," Oleg said.

"I was told there's a grace period for new residents—"

"At the discretion of the authorities," Oleg said, folding his arms. "Which means me."

The man blinked in disbelief. Zare couldn't meet his eyes.

"You're just a couple of kids."

"We are Imperial cadets, acting on behalf of Governor Pryce," Oleg snapped. "You're in violation of the law. I might allow you the grace period, but you have to give me something in return."

"Give you something? I don't understand."

"Tell me about your neighbors. Who's breaking the law?"

"There's nothing like that around here," the man stammered. "Just people trying to make a living."

"I don't believe you. Have any of your neighbors criticized the Empire or questioned government policy on Lothal?"

"That isn't against the law," the man said. Zare closed his eyes. He wanted to scream.

"Treason is most certainly illegal. As a citizen, it's your duty to report any violation of Imperial law."

"I understand that," the man said. "But—"

"It's obvious you *don't* understand," Oleg said, pulling out his datapad. "Let's see—'failure to register.'"

"Wait! Um . . . the bar on the corner? They bring in barrels of ebla beer at night. The barrels don't have tax stamps."

Oleg lowered his datapad. "And who brings these barrels?"

"A Dug in a speeder truck," the man said, looking around furtively. "I only saw it once, right at closing time."

"Now we're getting somewhere," Oleg said. "And

when you were at this bar, what did you hear your neighbors say about the Empire?"

Zare said nothing while Oleg finished interrogating the man, eventually allowing him to go back into his house after a firm warning that the Empire would check on his family's registrations. Then he turned to Zare, who was standing against the fence with his arms folded.

"Were you listening, Leonis?" Oleg asked. "That's how you do it."

"How you do what? Bully someone who's already helping the Empire so he doubts whether he should anymore?"

"What are you talking about?"

"That guy works for Sienar—he spends the day helping build TIE fighters. And you threatened to haul him to jail for not filling out a couple of stupid forms."

"He was breaking the law, Leonis," Oleg said. "And when I confronted him about that, he told me about a customs violation and three possibly treasonous statements."

"You found some untaxed barrels of beer. Congratulations, Nazhros—there should be a statue of you. Beating the Separatists was nothing compared to the blow you've struck against corruption on Lothal."

"And treason. Interesting how you forgot that part, Leonis."

"Oh, yeah—a few guys in a bar complained about the government. Never mind that there's no evidence they committed an actual crime."

"The statements are crime enough," Oleg said. "And we'll see how Captain Roddance feels about it. Remember what he said, Leonis—we're going to be judged on results now, not how good we are at jumping between platforms. And you're already behind."

When the cadets returned to the Academy, Zare was relieved to see Lieutenant Chiron standing alongside Roddance. The teams took turns recounting the results of their house-to-house searches. Cadets Uzall and Giles had earned the most points—a fugitive weapons smuggler had bolted from one of the houses in their grid and been apprehended by stormtroopers several blocks away. Oleg and Zare were second, thanks to a long list of small legal violations and treasonous rumors that Oleg had forced out of the people he'd interrogated.

"These are good numbers, Cadets Oleg and Leonis," Roddance said. "Though I understand most of the credit should go to Cadet Oleg."

Zare risked a glance sideways at Oleg, who was smiling back at Roddance. There was no way Roddance could have known who was responsible for their discoveries—unless Oleg had told him, probably over a private comlink channel. Clearly that was what had happened, but Roddance's reaction hadn't been to punish Oleg—it had been to praise him in front of the entire squad, and at Zare's expense.

Zare's eyes jumped to Chiron, who was staring back at him. The officer gave an almost imperceptible shake of his head.

"I found an interesting lead, sir," Oleg said. "Seems like evading customs taxes is a pretty active business in the neighborhood we searched. I heard a number of reports of goods being moved at night from a central warehouse."

Some of the other cadets muttered among themselves, and a few snickered.

"Silence in the ranks!" barked Roddance.

"Sir, regulation of trade is relatively new on Lothal," Chiron said. "As I understand it, until recently Governor Pryce addressed the issue of customs duties going unpaid through a program of educating citizens. She felt that was a better approach than fines and arrests."

Roddance eyed Chiron for a long moment.

"Surely you don't condone cheating the Empire out

of the credits it needs to ensure the safety and security of all citizens?" he asked.

"Of course not, sir," Chiron said. "I raised the issue in hopes that you'd explain to the cadets which violations of the law are most important to uncover and stop during the present operation."

"I see," Roddance said. He began to pace up and down the ranks of the cadets, studying each boy's or girl's face in turn.

"To answer your question, Lieutenant, *every* violation is important," Roddance snapped. "All trade must now be authorized. And we should remember that there are no victimless crimes. Every evasion of the law is an attack on the social order."

Chiron nodded slowly. His face was expressionless, but Zare could feel his misery—and his defiance. He'd finally been pushed too far.

"Sir?" Zare asked before he could think it through. "What about the reports we collected about citizens who questioned Imperial policy? What will be done with those?"

Roddance stood in front of Zare.

"They will be investigated, of course."

"I see, sir," Zare said. "And how much time will those investigations take, sir?"

"As much time as is required, Cadet Leonis."

"Thank you, sir. And what potential crimes won't be investigated while the authorities look into what somebody's neighbor might have said?"

That got the cadets murmuring among themselves. A smile twitched at the corners of Roddance's mouth, but his eyes were like ice.

"Are you questioning Imperial policy in this regard, Cadet Leonis?"

"Not at all, sir," Zare said. "That would be treasonous. I'm just trying to understand the overall mission. That's something we've been trained to do, sir."

"Then understand this, Leonis. Nothing is more important than Imperial law. *Nothing*. People define justice their own way, which leads to instability and friction. But everyone understands power and its ruthless, uniform application in support of the law. Enforcing that law is every cadet's duty. Is that clear?"

"Of course, sir."

"I hope so," Roddance said, backing up one step and surveying the cadets. "The strength of the Empire is more than blaster rifles and troop transports and Star Destroyers—it is *loyalty*. Disloyal thoughts among Imperial citizens are preludes to disloyal statements. And disloyal statements are preludes to disloyal actions. The earlier the Empire can break this treasonous chain, the more effectively it can prevent the disruption of order."

Roddance's eyes fell on Zare again.

"As Imperial cadets, your loyalties and associations have been investigated," he said. "From now on, there will be no allowances made for anything short of absolute loyalty to our Emperor and unquestioned devotion to our cause. Dismissed."

Merei slowed her jumpspeeder to a halt in front of Jix and waited for him to get flustered about having to climb on behind her and put his arms around her waist.

But this morning Jix just settled himself on the speeder and leaned against her. He didn't avert his yellow eyes, and his cheeks didn't flush a deeper blue.

Which Merei had to admit was a little disappointing.

"Did you hear the news?" Jix asked.

"No," Merei said. "What's happened?"

"The governor's crackdown is what happened. Stormtrooper squads launched raids all over Capital City in the middle of the night. They hit one of the boss's warehouses and two of his gambling clubs."

"Just our places?" Merei asked as she accelerated into traffic.

"No—everybody's," Jix said. "But the boss isn't happy. He owes credits to guys up the food chain, and now the flow of money has been disrupted."

"He must be having kittens," Merei muttered.

"By the litter."

But when Merei arrived at the Gray Syndicate's headquarters, Laxo looked up from his network terminal and gave her his usual grin.

"Busy morning, huh, kid? I assume Jix or one of those other little gossips caught you up on the night's events?"

When Merei hesitated, Laxo waved one pudgy hand dismissively.

"Saves me the trouble of explaining it for the eight millionth time," he said. "Now listen up. Get on your speeder and go visit Durchine, Holshef, Apapaba, Kinlo, and Marhas. Tell them Rosey will come by and move them to new hiding places tonight, in case more informants are wagging their rotten little tongues. I want them all packed and ready when Rosey arrives."

"You forgot Pinson," Merei said. Pinson was a small-time grifter whom Laxo had stashed on the top floor of a warehouse near the spaceport.

"Nah, I didn't forget Pinson. You don't need to worry about him anymore."

"What happened to him? Did he get pinched?"

"Something like that," Laxo said with a yawn. "I sold him to a bounty hunter."

"What?"

"You heard me. Got a cut of the bounty, too."

"You can't do that!" Merei sputtered. "You promised to protect him! He paid you to protect him!"

"And I did," Laxo said. "He got seven extra months of freedom, didn't he? Look, kid, it's just business. It reached the point where there were more credits to be made with Pinson in Imperial hands than there were hiding him. Simple as that."

"I see," Merei said, seething. "And what about the others? What about Holshef?"

Laxo smiled.

"Ah, yes, the friendly neighborhood poet. He can still pay, so no need to change his status."

Merei nodded, her face grim.

"So is this the way it's going to be from now on?"

Laxo sighed.

"I thought you were smart," he said. "This is the way it's *always* been. My power doesn't come from that pistol Rosey's cleaning over there, but from the information I've collected. To retain that power, I'm always thinking about how to maximize the value of that

113

information. If that means keeping it a secret, great. And if it means sharing it with the Empire, then that's what I do."

Laxo smiled at her, then waggled his fingers in dismissal. Merei's hands were shaking as she descended the stairs. She'd understood his message all too clearly: sooner or later, he'd sell her out, too.

When the cadets returned from the second day of the Imperial crackdown, Zare remained silent as he put his gear away. Then he left the barracks and walked down the hall to stand outside of Chiron's office.

Am I doing the right thing? Zare wondered.

It was a dangerous step. He knew that much. But he had to tell somebody—and Chiron had left no doubt the day before that he disapproved of the Empire's methods.

Zare pressed the chime and took a deep breath as the black door slid into the wall. Chiron was sitting behind his desk, his cap in his hands. He looked up at Zare, frowning, then waved him in.

"Were you briefed on today's mission, sir?" Zare asked, hating the quaver in his voice as he asked the question.

"I was," Chiron said. "I'm sorry I couldn't brief you and your fellow cadets about it in advance. I saw from the duty roster that you were paired with Cadet Oleg again."

Zare nodded.

"Sir—" he began, but stopped when Chiron shook his head emphatically, raising his eyes toward the ceiling.

Zare felt dizzy for a moment. Had the Empire grown so paranoid that it had begun spying on its own officers?

"Come with me, Cadet Leonis," Chiron said, getting to his feet. "I have an answer to that question about troop-transport maintenance that you asked. But it's simpler just to show you."

They walked through the main hangar and into the plaza outside the Academy, lit by the last rays of the setting sun. Chiron didn't stop until they were a good twenty meters away from the massive blast doors.

"All right, Zare, now tell me about today," Chiron said.

Zare looked around the plaza. This was where he'd pretended to try to shoot Jai Kell and Dev Morgan as they'd fled.

Chiron looked down at him, waiting. Zare wondered what the lieutenant was thinking. He'd stopped Zare from saying something that might have gotten the cadet in trouble, but why had he done that? Yesterday wasn't the first time Chiron had disagreed with the Empire's policies, but he'd always made it clear that he would support them anyway. Had that changed? Zare felt a wild surge of hope at the idea, at the possibility that Chiron might be able to help him.

Then he pushed the thought away. He had to be very careful. Chiron had no idea about his past. And for Zare's own safety, it had to stay that way.

"I don't know where to begin, sir," Zare said.

"Just begin," Chiron said. "You can speak freely here."

Zare nodded.

"They . . . they made us take away children," he said.

"The children of fugitives with warrants for their arrest," Chiron said.

Zare nodded.

"And what did they tell you about the purpose of the mission?"

"That taking the children into protective custody would make the fugitives turn themselves in."

"And how did the operation go?"

"The children were frightened," Zare said, his hands balling into fists. "And their guardians were frantic. We had to arrest some of them."

Chiron stared across the plaza at the lights of the city.

"Was anyone hurt?" he asked.

"No," Zare said. "But . . . I understand these are fugitives, sir, but the children aren't responsible for what their mothers or fathers did. *They* didn't do anything wrong."

He had thought about refusing the order the moment Captain Roddance delivered it. But he had said nothing. Refusing an order was grounds for expulsion from the Academy. If he did that, he'd never get to Arkanis—and, he'd realized helplessly, the loss of one cadet would do nothing to stop the operation.

Roddance had explained that the cadets were being used for this operation because he figured they could handle a few kids. Zare had felt a chill at the curt, callous way he said it—and at how Oleg insisted on keeping his faceplate down while he barked orders. Zare had taken his helmet off entirely, inviting the children to try it on. He'd tried to turn the terrible day into a game of sorts—a chance to ride in a troop transport and see how it worked.

When Zare was finished, Chiron put his hand on the cadet's shoulder.

"I'm as appalled as you are, Zare," he said, his voice tight with anger. "But Agent Kallus's orders were quite specific. For what it's worth, I can assure you the children will be well cared for."

"But not by people they know," Zare said bitterly.

"You know that doesn't make any of this right, sir."

"No, it doesn't," Chiron said. "Roddance is gunning for you, Zare. That's why you were teamed up with Oleg again. This crackdown of the governor's is the perfect opportunity to provoke you into doing something that will get you kicked out of the Academy."

Zare had suspected as much but was still alarmed at this confirmation of his fears.

"I was foolish yesterday, challenging Captain Roddance the way I did," Chiron muttered. "I apologize for it. I'm trying to protect you, Zare, but there are limits to what I can do."

Chiron hesitated. "Can I trust you to keep a secret, Zare?"

Zare nodded, thinking glumly of how many secrets he had kept from Chiron.

"I've recommended that you be transferred to Arkanis for the fall, and Sergeant Currahee has seconded that recommendation," he said. "And Commandant Aresko has approved the transfer. He hasn't forgotten your efforts on behalf of your fellow cadets."

Zare's gaze swung back toward the hangar, where he'd taken control of an AT-DP. He could barely breathe: the path to Arkanis and his sister was open to him.

"Captain Roddance doesn't agree, and that's why

he has you in his sights," Chiron said urgently. "But he can't do anything unless you do something rash—such as fighting again with Oleg or disobeying a direct order. Don't give him an opening."

Chiron looked out across the plaza.

"Arkanis will be different, Zare," he said. "There isn't any of the social unrest there that plagues Lothal, which has led to this unfortunate overreaction. On Arkanis you'll be able to become the exemplary Imperial officer I know you can be."

Zare stiffened. Chiron was practically pleading with him, unaware that everything Zare had done as a cadet was under false pretenses.

"I've known you could be such an officer since the moment I saw you, Zare," Chiron said. "But you have to hold on a little longer. Please tell me you can do that."

Zare forced himself to look Chiron in the eye and nod. The officer smiled.

"That's a relief, cadet. And I think that concludes our lesson in troop-transport maintenance."

"Yes, sir," Zare said.

But as they walked back through the hangar, Zare felt sick to his stomach. People had been telling him to hold on for the better part of a year now, first at AppSci and now at the Academy. And he had done so.

But he'd never imagined having to interrogate Imperial citizens and take away children. And hadn't the Empire done that to his own parents? Dhara's disappearance had left a gaping hole in the Leonis family. And now he was helping the Empire do the same thing to other families.

Recently he'd been able to think of little besides how to rescue Dhara. But wasn't there a point where the damage done to innocent people became more important than his quest? And if that happened—if it already *had* happened—what was the right thing for him to do?

Merei didn't need to work the dinnertime conversation around to the latest developments in her mother's investigation; Jessa Spanjaf did it for her.

"We've narrowed down the intrusion pattern from the Transportation Ministry to three repeater services," she said. "I'll file a request for a search warrant with the Justice Ministry tomorrow morning."

"How long?" Merei asked.

"We'll ask them to expedite it," Jessa said with a shrug. "Given the current crackdown, it won't be a problem. I'd say we'll have the account data from those services within two or three days."

"And how long will it take after that to find the intruder?" Merei asked, staring at her plate.

"Once we have the account data, you mean? Seconds."

"And then it's game over for our intruder," Gandr said with a smile.

"Well, not quite," Jessa said. "If they had any brains at all, they logged in from a café or a rented room or someplace relatively hard to connect to someone. At that point it will be back to police work—security cams and rental records. But in a couple of days, we can get back to normal life."

Merei got up from the table, stacking her utensils on her plate with a clatter.

"Everything okay, Mer Bear?" her father asked.

"I've just got a lot of work," she muttered, fleeing into the kitchen.

She put the dishes in the washer, retreated upstairs to her bedroom, then shut the door and stared at the screen of her network terminal, blank except for a clock in the corner. Zare would be in the mess hall. His evening free period wouldn't start for fifteen minutes or so.

It was one of the three days of the week he was allowed to comm with family and friends. Merei typed the first half of a message to him, then stopped and cleared it. She wouldn't be able to tell him anything. He'd notice that she was distressed, but he'd have no idea why. And of course he was so wrapped up in his own problems that he barely had time to consider hers.

She entered a different comm code. Jix answered immediately, peering at his screen.

"Hey, Merei," he said, his face breaking into a smile. "What's going on?"

"Oh, you know—just enjoying my final days before prison."

"Ha-ha," Jix said. "Yeah, I'm really worried about exams, too! Say, let me comm you back. It'll only take a sec."

The screen went blank. A moment later Jix was back.

"We're encrypted," he said, his voice tinny and faintly metallic. "Now tell me what's happening."

Merei watched Jix's expression turn grave as she told him what had happened.

"You have to ask Laxo for help," he said. "I know you don't want to, but you're valuable to him. And he likes you."

Merei shook her head. Any chance that she'd ask Laxo for help had vanished the previous day, when the crime boss had told her he'd sold Pinson. If she went to Laxo, perhaps he would help her. After all, she knew he had dealings with everybody in Lothal's black market. But then he'd own her forever.

And perhaps he wouldn't help her at all. He was always calculating values and risks. Perhaps he'd run the numbers in his head and decide to make her disappear before the Empire could interrogate her.

"No, Jix," she said. "I can't do that."

"What are you going to do, then?"

"I don't know," Merei said.

She'd considered and rejected any number of ideas—telling her parents, turning herself in and claiming she'd only wanted to help Zare at the Academy, or using her savings on a ticket off-world. They all seemed like different ways to ruin her life.

"I do have one idea," Jix said. "It's super risky, which is why I haven't brought it up before. But so is everything else at this point. Do you know what a pulse-mag is?"

"Of course," Merei said. "It's used to erase data."

"Right. Laxo lent me one so I could . . . well, never mind. Anyway, I've got it. It's pretty small—fits in my carryall."

"What are you thinking?"

"That we go to Bakiska's. You bluff your way in, saying that you're there on business for Laxo. Then we use the pulse-mag to scramble the data on the machine with your account information."

Merei pursed her lips, drumming her fingers on the desk.

"That won't work, though," she said. "They've got to

have dozens of machines in there—we don't have any idea which one is the right one."

Jix grinned.

"Actually, I do. I called in a few favors. I found out where the machine warehousing Bakiska's inactive and deleted accounts is."

Merei looked down. Jix really had been working hard to help her.

"You okay?"

"I'm fine," she said, smiling at him. "Thank you, Jix. Pick you up at V-SIS at 0700?"

Merei sat at her desk for a few minutes, thinking. Whoever ran Bakiska's would discover the damage quickly and make a scene with Laxo. The boss would be furious, but she was willing to weather that storm. If Jix's idea succeeded, Laxo's hold on her would be much weaker.

It's not the greatest plan in the world, but it's the best I can come up with, she thought.

She wondered what Zare would say. She put her head down on her arms, thinking about the sound of his voice, the way his eyes would widen when he was amused, the smooth confidence in the way he moved. And all at once she had to see his face.

She'd expected to have to leave a message, but Zare answered immediately. He was in one of the little comm rooms the cadets could use.

"Zare, are you all right?" she asked, forgetting for a moment that their communications were monitored. "You look terrible."

"I'm fine," Zare said. "Just been another long day. We're assisting with Governor Pryce's efforts to improve security and citizen safety in Capital City."

Before the monitoring began, Merei would have instantly asked what that meant. Now all she could do was nod. Zare's dark brown skin was gray with exhaustion, and his eyes were red. He had his elbows on the desk and rested his head in his hands, shutting his eyes for a moment.

Zare was the one she'd trusted to help her through crises like the one she faced now, Merei thought. But now there was no way he could help her. She couldn't even ask.

"I wasn't expecting you," he said. "I came in here to call my parents. Mom's birthday is tomorrow."

"Oh. I'm sorry. You should do that."

"No, it's fine. I was just surprised."

They looked at each other. Merei wanted to tell him everything. It felt like the words were piling up inside her, taking up so much space that they needed to tumble out. But there was no way to do that. The Empire had taken away their ability to talk to each other, and when they could meet, they felt like strangers.

"Zare . . ." Merei said, then stopped, not wanting to continue but knowing she had to.

He raised his eyes and just looked at her.

"I can't do this anymore," she said quietly. She felt the tears leaking out of her eyes and brushed irritably at them, then gave up and let them run down her cheeks.

Zare stared down at his lap, then looked away. His chest rose and fell, and then he nodded, still not looking at her.

"I'm sorry," Merei said. "I . . . I want to see you so badly. I want to be able to talk to you, like we used to. But we can't. We can't, and I can't take it anymore."

"I understand," Zare said, and gave her a small smile. But she could see the hurt in his eyes.

"I wish things were different," he said, and his throat bobbed up and down. "I wish *everything* was different."

It was dim inside the troop transport as it made its way across the outskirts of Capital City—dim and quiet. On a different morning, Zare might have found it tempting to close his eyes and sleep, lulled by the thrum of the repulsorlifts.

But that was impossible this morning. There was no way Zare could sleep with Oleg's eyes on him, knowing that any second they'd get their orders for the day.

Oleg smirked at Zare, who ignored him—just as he'd ignored him when Roddance once again paired them together for the day's operations. He simply waited.

Zare wasn't sure when he'd made up his mind. It might have been while staring at the ceiling of the barracks, or in the shower, or while waiting in the chow line at the mess hall. But at some point he'd reached a decision: he wasn't taking any more children away from their parents.

And if that meant he was dismissed as a cadet or lost his chance to transfer to Arkanis, then so be it.

I'll find you some other way, Dhara, he thought. *But I won't do any more evil in the name of the Emperor.*

Lost in thought, he was slow to react when their datapads chimed. Oleg read their orders first and chuckled.

Supplymaster Lyste's agents had investigated Oleg's tip about customs duties being evaded and concluded that goods were being stockpiled in a warehouse for distribution in that part of Capital City. Roddance had assigned a squad of stormtroopers to the raid and put Oleg in charge, with Zare ordered to assist him.

Zare had to smile: Roddance wasn't even trying to hide his efforts on Oleg's behalf now. He was conscious of the other cadet's eyes on him and knew Oleg was disappointed by his lack of a reaction. But it didn't matter. Zare had done his best to impersonate the perfect cadet, but the act could go no further. There was nothing to do but wait for the order he knew was coming, the one he would refuse to obey.

Jix was waiting with his collar up around his neck against the cold. Patting his carryall, he smiled nervously at Merei as she pulled up on her jumpspeeder.

"The pulse-mag's got a containment field," Jix said. "So don't worry, it won't mess up your speeder's onboard systems."

"That's good," Merei said. "I'd hate to push my ride all the way to Lower Gallo."

As they zipped across the city, Merei could sense that Jix was nervous. He kept shifting his weight and turning his head from side to side behind her. But she felt oddly calm. This was the day she'd extricate herself from Laxo's web or face the consequences. It was dangerous—so dangerous her mind shrank from considering it—but at least she was doing something instead of just waiting to run out of time.

They pulled up outside a modular building on a nondescript street filled with tapcafs and diners that catered to everyone from bureaucrats to speeder-truck drivers making cargo runs across Lothal. A holographic sign advertised strong caf, fast data connections, and no questions asked—which made Bakiska's much the same as many of Capital City's dodgier info-houses.

"Let me do the talking," Merei said, and Jix nodded, his eyes wide. She hoped he was ready for this, then tried not to laugh. Not so long ago, the idea of what she was about to try would have left her sick with fear. But she'd been on dozens of errands for Laxo since then. She'd been threatened and abused and had blasters pointed at her, and she had learned to do her job despite it all.

A young woman with elaborate tattoos and cybernetic implants sat behind the front desk. She eyed them with vague interest.

"Gray Syndicate," Merei said, and the woman sat up in her chair, back stiffening. "People are talking about your data security—the boss sent us over to check it out."

"Our techs aren't in this early," the woman said. "Maybe in an hour—"

"That's why I came over now—I don't need or want your techs. I'll use my own eyes and draw my own conclusions. It's that way, right?"

"Let me get on the comm. The boss—"

"No time for that," Merei said, inclining her head at

Jix and striding past the desk. "If everything checks out I'll be on my way in a few minutes."

"You can't do that!" the woman called after them.

Jix nodded at a hallway partially obscured by a curtain, and Merei headed that way as the woman yelled for them to stop.

"Walk faster," she said to Jix. "When you see the machine, hit it with the pulse-mag. Don't listen to anybody—I'll handle them."

For a few seconds she thought they were going to make it. But then another door along the corridor opened, and a hulking, bald Iotran stepped into their path, blaster raised.

"Gray Syndicate," Merei said. "Boss sent us to check out your security."

"Don't care if you're the red Royal Guard," the Iotran rumbled. "Take another step and you'll be two smoking spots."

Two more thugs stepped into the hallway, grabbing Merei and Jix. One of them wrestled Jix's satchel away and opened it, removing the pulse-mag.

"And where were you going with that?" asked a voice with a Core Worlds accent.

The voice belonged to a pale human woman with spiky white hair. She walked slowly down the hallway toward them, eyeing the pulse-mag.

"I know who you are," she said, taking the satchel and jamming the pulse-mag back into it. "You're Laxo's new courier."

"That's right," Merei said, shoulders sagging in relief. "He asked me to run a surprise security check."

"With a pulse-mag?"

"That's for another job," Jix said. "We only need a minute."

The white-haired woman smiled icily.

"You're not getting ten seconds in my data center—not after you came in with that thing," she said. "If you didn't work for Laxo, no one would ever see the two of you alive again."

She thrust the satchel back into Jix's arms.

"Tell your boss whatever security concerns he has about my place, he can work them out with me—not by arranging some kind of school field trip. No, never mind—I'll tell him that myself. Now get out of here."

The thugs marched them outside and stood in the doorway until Merei and Jix had climbed on her jump-speeder and zoomed away.

"Now what do we do?" Jix wailed in her ear.

Merei said nothing as she pulled into the loading zone for a commuter speeder bus.

"This is our stop," she said.

Jix got off the speeder, looking puzzled.

"Go to V-SIS, Jix," Merei said. "Don't come to headquarters anymore. You need to lie low."

"Why? What are you doing?"

"It's better that you don't know."

"But I want to help you."

"You can—by letting me borrow that pulse-mag. But I need to do the rest of this myself."

Jix handed over the satchel.

"I don't understand what you have in mind."

Merei leaned forward and touched his cheek.

"I know, and I'm sorry. But it's for the best."

The troop transport came to a halt, and Oleg scrambled to his feet, lowering his faceplate and waving impatiently for Zare to follow him. Outside, the sun was still low in the sky, and the morning air was cold on Zare's face. Six stormtroopers had deployed from their side racks and stood in line in front of a warehouse, waiting for Oleg's instructions.

"Our informant tells us they bring cargo shortly before dawn, catalog it, and distribute it at night," Oleg said over the squad's shared channel. "Let's catch 'em napping."

"Cadet Oleg?" Zare asked.

Oleg turned, and Zare knew he was scowling behind his armored mask.

"What is it, Leonis?"

"I have a question to ensure we're properly prepared for this mission," Zare said. "What cargo are they housing? Is it something dangerous, such as spice or weapons?"

The stormtroopers exchanged glances behind their helmets.

"Not as far as we know, cadet," Oleg said. "It's a case of customs evasion. But surely you recall that all trade must be registered—and that every violation of the law is an attack on society. Or is it that you think you're too good for this mission, cadet?"

"Of course not," Zare said, then smiled. "It's an honor, Cadet Oleg. What could be more important work for servants of the Empire than looking for tax stamps?"

Oleg stepped so close to Zare that his helmet nearly touched Zare's nose.

"That's the thing about you and your kind, Leonis," he said. "You think you can pick and choose which laws to enforce. And you want to do that because it makes you other people's master. The only fair system is one where everyone is equal before the law and where the law is absolute, with neither fear nor favor. And that's the system you're going to enforce today. Or I'll have you before Agent Kallus himself. Now is that clear?"

"Absolutely. Captain Roddance couldn't have said it better."

Oleg stared at him. Zare could hear the stormtroopers shifting in their armor.

"Well, Cadet Oleg?" Zare asked. "I believe this mission is under your command?"

"That's correct. We're going in. If they don't open this door, blast it apart."

He strutted over to the comm button and depressed it.

"Open this door," Oleg demanded. "In the name of the Empire."

The door opened and the stormtroopers marched inside, followed a moment later by Oleg and Zare. Inside, a small group of workers and droids stood glumly with their hands raised, surrounded by crates and barrels.

"Surely we can work this out," grunted a bald-headed, black-eyed Bith worker. "There's an arrangement."

"It's just been canceled," Oleg said, turning to two of the stormtroopers. "Search the rest of the premises. I want any stragglers brought here. Leonis, inspect those barrels."

Zare turned several barrels around, then tipped them over on their sides.

"Customs stamps?" Oleg asked.

Zare shook his head. "No sign they've been inspected or taxed."

"Just as we were told. Open that one."

Zare cracked the seal on one of the barrels, then tilted it so Oleg could see inside. It was full of grain.

Oleg nodded, then cracked open his faceplate. He was beaming.

"We're confiscating it all," he told the stormtroopers. "Arrest these workers."

The two other stormtroopers returned from the warehouse office, with two men walking between them. Zare peered at the new arrivals in puzzlement. Something about them seemed familiar.

"Nazhros?" one of them asked.

Oleg's jaw dropped. The men were his uncles—the ones who had sent him to the Academy, and came to see him on Visiting Day.

"Um, there's been a mistake," Oleg told the storm-trooper commander. "Release these two. Cadet Leonis, reseal that barrel."

The stormtroopers exchanged puzzled glances. Their helmets turned in Zare's direction.

Oleg stared at Zare. His mouth moved, but no sound came out. Zare lowered his faceplate.

"You have your orders," Zare told the stormtroopers. "These men have broken Imperial law. Take them into custody. And, Cadet Oleg? You're relieved of duty."

After Merei dropped off Jix, she found a quiet intersection on the edge of town, shut off her jumpspeeder's engine, and recorded a message on her comlink. She checked it, then set it to transmit to her parents' channels in fifteen minutes. Then she fired up her speeder and headed for the Gray Syndicate's headquarters.

Her comlink chimed. For a moment she was afraid she'd set the timer wrong on the message she'd just recorded. But it wasn't either of her parents' message IDs. She wanted to ignore the call but feared it would be Jix. He might need to be talked out of doing something brave and foolish.

"What?" she demanded.

"Is this Merei-1?" rumbled a voice. "It's your old pal Spectre-4."

Merei pulled over. She recognized the voice of the big purple-skinned alien who'd been part of the operation outside the Imperial Academy, the one the mysterious Dev Morgan had been part of. Merei and Spectre-5—a slim girl in Mandalorian armor—had taken turns using the decoder Dev and Zare had stolen.

"I'm a little busy right now," she said, conscious of the message that would soon be delivered. "What do you want?"

"We need your boyfriend's help," Spectre-4 rumbled. "We need to get in touch with Zare."

"He's not my—Never mind. That's impossible."

"Even if resistance to the Empire on Lothal might be at stake?"

Merei stared at her comlink in disbelief.

"You can't contact him—not since the Empire started monitoring all Academy communications," she said. Then her voice rose with fury: "I don't care what's at stake—you need to leave Zare alone! Don't you understand the danger he's in?"

"That I do, missy," the alien said. "My compatriots and I face it every day of our lives."

Merei thought of the alien and the girl in the alley, hiding from the stormtroopers. And Zare in the Academy, trying to keep everyone from figuring out he wasn't what he appeared to me. And Dhara as she was led away from her fellow cadets, with no idea why. And she thought of herself, forced into an improvised plan as her mother's hunters closed in.

"If you need Zare that badly, send the droid," she snapped. "That's what you did last time."

She shut off the comlink and brought her jump-speeder to a halt a few blocks from Laxo's headquarters, then walked the rest of the way. The thugs guarding the alley behind the tavern stepped aside without so much as a glance at the satchel under her arm. She walked down the filthy alley, squeezing past the white speeder van, then reached into her pocket and activated the locator her father had given her. Then she banged on the dented door.

It opened. A burly Aqualish in the kitchen nodded at her as she walked by, her heart thudding in her chest. She was relieved to see that none of Laxo's slicers had arrived yet. A couple of thugs were playing sabacc while Rosey sat nearby, checking the contacts on her blaster's power cell.

"The boss thought you might show up," Rosey muttered. "Don't know what you did, but he's madder than a starved rancor."

"Yeah, I figured," Merei said, thinking of the pulse-mag in her carryall and the locator in her pocket, steadily transmitting her whereabouts.

Rosey turned back to inspecting her power cell. Merei thought about urging the Rodian to flee, but she knew she couldn't. Her plan was desperate enough as it was.

Rosey looked up and saw Merei studying her.

"Hey, kid, if he gives me the order . . . well, remember it's nothing personal," she said.

"Right, Rosey," she said, looking away. "Nothing personal. Just business."

Merei hurried up the stairs, trying to calculate the distance between her house and Laxo's headquarters. She found the crime boss sitting behind his network terminal. He was wearing a robe and his lilac slippers and sipping caf.

"I was worried I might have to send Rosey to dig you out of a hole somewhere," Laxo said. "I respect that you came on your own, at least."

Merei nodded, her eyes drifting to the data tower below Laxo's desk—the one that contained all of the Gray Syndicate's records.

Laxo sighed.

"I can't figure out what you two idiots were doing at Bakiska's. Do you know what a headache that's caused me this morning, kid? As if I don't have enough problems already. Lost another warehouse to the Empire, and now this."

Laxo shook his head, then closed his eyes, pinching the bridge of his nose. Suddenly Merei felt guilty. He was angry with her, but not angry enough to have Rosey make her disappear. He was going to let her off with a lecture and some kind of punishment—because in his own weird way, he was fond of her.

And she was about to repay him by sending him to prison.

Laxo opened his eyes. They were like chips of ice.

"I just sold Holshef to a bounty hunter," he said. "The hunter will be here in an hour. You're going to take him to your poet friend's latest hideout—Rosey moved him to 1044 Chapel—and stay while he collects the bounty. And next time you think about crossing me, you'll remember what it felt like watching that."

Someone yelled out a warning downstairs. Laxo got to his feet just as the translucent windows exploded. Stormtroopers landed amid the chunks of shattered glass, having descended cables from a gunship above.

Merei screamed and ducked behind Laxo's desk. The crime boss took a reflexive step backward and stumbled over her, dropping his mug. Merei yanked the pulse-mag out of her bag, activated it, and jammed it against Laxo's data tower.

He'll say that I worked for him, but without his records there won't be any proof, Merei thought. *It will be his word against mine. He'll go to prison, but the rest of his people can disappear. And I'll make it up to him somehow.*

Blaster bolts filled the air, and Merei smelled ozone. Then Laxo's body crashed down into the chair next to her.

No! This wasn't supposed to happen!

The firing had stopped. One of Laxo's lilac slippers lay on the floor next to his empty mug. Merei tried to make her mind work. Had Laxo reached for a blaster, or did one of the troopers panic? Did the firing start downstairs or in the office?

She couldn't remember. Everything had happened at once, faster than she could follow. She couldn't catch her breath, and her hands wouldn't stop shaking.

"Come on out, kid," said a stormtrooper's voice. "You're safe now."

Merei dropped the pulse-mag and scrambled out from behind the desk, away from Laxo's body.

"Your mother got the message they made you send," the stormtrooper commander said. "The one saying you'd been kidnapped and they'd kill you if she didn't call off the investigation. Your locator led us right to you—good thing they didn't find it."

Merei managed to nod.

"Downstairs?" she asked, thinking of Rosey.

"We cleaned the whole nest out—they never knew what hit them," the stormtrooper said, sounding pleased. "Like I said, you're safe."

Merei couldn't stop shivering. She turned and saw Laxo's lifeless eyes staring at her, his expression bewildered.

What have I done?

Hands shook Zare awake. He gasped and shoved them away, adrenaline shooting through him.

"Easy, Leonis," the squat figure of Currahee said from where she stood next to Zare's bunk. "Get dressed—Captain Roddance wants you in his office immediately."

Zare dressed hastily as the other cadets stirred in sleepy confusion. Oleg's bunk was empty.

When he entered Roddance's office, the captain was standing beside his desk, holding a cup of caf. Zare saw the ill-concealed unease on his hard, angular face—and then he saw why Roddance looked wary.

A tall figure in black was standing behind Roddance's desk, looking out the window into the pre-dawn gloom of a winter morning on Lothal. He was bald, with skin like gray stone.

It was the Inquisitor—just like in his dream.

Roddance glanced momentarily at the silent figure, then decided not to interrupt his vigil.

"I hope yesterday was a lesson about the value of loyalty," Roddance said. "Cadet Oleg failed that test—he was an associate of those who thought themselves above the law. This Empire has no room for liars and traitors—or for those who fail to realize lies and treason are just points along the same line."

"Oleg didn't know about his uncles, sir," Zare said, surprised to find himself defending the boy he loathed and who loathed him.

Roddance's eyes jumped to the silent Inquisitor, then back to Zare.

"It doesn't matter," Roddance snapped. "His associations were a weakness that enemies of the Empire might have exploited. To serve the Empire, one must purge oneself of all such weaknesses."

"Including compassion?" Zare asked.

The Inquisitor turned, his burning yellow eyes fixed on Zare. One corner of his mouth twitched upward. Zare's mind shrank from contemplating what such a being would find amusing.

"Compassion," the Inquisitor drawled, "is the most insidious weakness of all. But we aren't here to discuss other cadets, Leonis. Your time at this academy is at an end."

Zare stared at the gray-skinned being in shock. The hairs on his neck rose, and he tried to suppress his fear, lest the Inquisitor sense it.

"I don't understand, sir," Zare said.

"Don't you?" the Inquisitor asked, then glanced at Roddance. "You may leave us, Captain."

Roddance exited his office with impressive speed. The door shut behind him, and those burning eyes turned back to Zare.

"You're being transferred to the academy on Arkanis," the Inquisitor said.

"You mean next year, sir?" Zare asked in astonishment.

"I mean as soon as it's processed."

I'm going to Arkanis.

Zare could barely think. He had despaired of winning that promotion and wondered how he could endure an entire spring and summer of waiting, even if he succeeded. And then he had given up, deciding that he couldn't continue to harm others—because Dhara might no longer be on Arkanis, or even alive.

And now, just like that, he was going there.

The Inquisitor watched those emotions playing over Zare's face.

"Thank you, sir," Zare said, belatedly trying to force himself back into the role of model Imperial cadet. "I'm honored to serve the Emperor."

"Who could doubt the commitment of such a promising young cadet?" the Inquisitor asked, and Zare lowered his eyes, too frightened to meet that terrible gaze.

Had that been mockery in the cultured voice? Had the Inquisitor seen through his act, his increasingly desperate deception?

Think of nothing think of nothing THINK OF NOTHING!

"Look at me, cadet," the Inquisitor said in a low growl, and Zare could feel that cruel mind reaching for his.

His chin rose of its own accord, until his eyes met the Inquisitor's. He felt like he was falling into those twin tunnels of fire.

"I'm looking forward to your training on Arkanis, Leonis," the Inquisitor said. "Your service to the Imperial cause will be more important than even you have hoped."

To Zare's surprise, Sergeant Currahee was waiting outside Roddance's office.

"Congratulations, Leonis," she said, then her mouth briefly contorted in what he suspected was an actual smile. "Now come with me."

Zare followed her through the corridors of Imperial headquarters in a daze.

"You're being upgraded to a class-three intel/courier clearance," Currahee said. "You'll need it on Arkanis."

"Yes, ma'am," Zare mumbled. "What's it like, ma'am? Arkanis, I mean."

"Never been there."

"Oh," Zare said. He couldn't focus; his thoughts kept snapping back to Arkanis and his sister. And the Inquisitor. What had he seen when he'd held Zare's eyes, back in Roddance's office? What did he know?

It was barely dawn; the corridors were nearly deserted except for a scattering of astromechs and mouse droids, beeping quietly to themselves as they pursued their daily errands.

Currahee took him to the security office, where a bug-eyed Imperial protocol droid regarded the two of them suspiciously before handing over a code cylinder.

"Don't lose it, Leonis—the replacement forms are a nightmare," Currahee said. "Welcome to class three."

"Thank you, ma'am," Zare muttered.

Currahee nodded, and that time it was definitely true: the corners of her mouth had twitched. Then she strode away.

"Do you require anything else, cadet?" the protocol droid grumbled after a moment.

"No," Zare said. "No, I'm fine."

He tucked the rank cylinder into his pocket and began the walk back to the barracks, still dazed. An astromech whistled, and he glanced at it absentmind-edly, checking to make sure the cylinder was still where he had put it.

Something bumped into him from behind, and he nearly stumbled. He turned, puzzled. It was the astromech that had whistled, a black model—

Dev Morgan's droid!

Zare looked around warily and crouched down next to the astromech. The droid tapped one of the utility doors on its chassis with a grasper arm, honking grump-ily. He opened the door and found a rolled-up piece of paper. Unfurling it revealed a hasty scrawl.

Meet me outside this evening. Tell the droid what time. Find out anything you can about imminent actions. It's life and death.

Zare looked around in disbelief, expecting to hear the clatter of stormtrooper armor. What if the Inquisitor had sensed the presence of Dev and his friends? What if he'd come here to await them and Zare was part of his trap?

The droid whistled at him.

But surely the Inquisitor had other reasons for returning to Lothal. Life and death, Dev had said. He and his friends weren't fools. They had to be desperate to risk contacting him this way.

Zare patted his pockets, and the droid hooted, extending a stylus with another arm. Zare took it and wrote a quick message on the back of the note, then gave paper and stylus to the droid. It tucked them inside its chassis and rolled away, clucking derisively to itself.

"Zare?"

Zare whirled to see Lieutenant Chiron walking down the corridor toward him.

"At ease, cadet," Chiron said with a chuckle. "Didn't mean to startle you. What did that droid want?"

"The droid? Oh. I . . . uh, dropped my code cylinder, sir. It saw it happen and whistled for me to stop."

"It bumped into you, you mean."

Zare stared at Chiron. If he'd seen everything that had just happened . . .

"It got black paint on the back of your uniform pants," Chiron said, smiling again. "Must have just gotten a touch-up at the repair shop."

"Oh," Zare said. "Yeah, I guess I wasn't really focusing, sir."

"I don't blame you, Zare. I came to offer my congratulations."

And then he was shaking Zare's hand, his smile broad.

"You've been through a lot this year, Cadet Leonis,"

Chiron said. "The disappearance of your sister, the attack on the Academy, the . . . *demands* placed on all of us by the recent security crackdown. And through it all you've performed your duty admirably. I'm glad that others have noticed what I saw from the beginning."

"Thank you, sir," Zare said, lowering his eyes. Chiron's kind words were genuine. He had always tried to help Zare.

"Headed back to the barracks?" Chiron asked.

"Yes, sir," Zare said. "It's nearly dawn. Reveille will be soon."

"Go, then," Chiron said. "Back to *bed*. I've cleared your duties for the day. Surely your parents will want to see you before you go."

Zare nodded. Of course they would. And Merei . . . but no. He had been so wrapped up in himself that he'd lost Merei. And now he couldn't think of a way to undo that.

Chiron was still smiling down at him, Zare realized.

"I'll do that—I'll go see my folks," he said, then saluted and forced himself to smile. "Thank you, sir. It's been a pleasure serving under you, sir."

"The pleasure, Zare, was all mine."

As Chiron walked off toward his office, Zare sighed and let his shoulders slump. He didn't know what awaited him on Arkanis, but he was glad that soon he'd no longer have to mislead the one man at the Academy who'd always been kind to him.

Sleep proved elusive. Zare had arrived after reveille, which meant he had to endure the good-natured taunts of his fellow cadets, followed by their handshakes, back slaps, and quick hugs. After they departed he lay in his bunk, staring at the featureless ceiling. But the silence was unfamiliar and slightly unnerving. He realized he'd never been in the barracks by himself.

Now that the Inquisitor was gone, the fog in his mind was lifting, and Zare's wariness slowly ebbed, to be replaced by a giddy disbelief. Surely his worries were nothing but paranoia. The Empire wouldn't give class-three clearance to a cadet suspected of treason. Roddance and Oleg had tried to break him, and they'd nearly succeeded. But in the end, Oleg had engineered his own downfall, and Roddance had seen Zare snatched away from him.

Zare had passed the Empire's tests and earned his reward.

Not long after sunset, Zare donned his helmet and walked through the Academy's main hangar, clicking his code cylinder when two stormtroopers stopped him at the exit. The soldiers nodded behind their armored masks and stepped aside, leaving Zare free to walk out into an unseasonably warm evening on Lothal.

Zare strode across the plaza outside the Academy, then turned and entered an alley. He heard something behind a stack of old crates and whirled around. A cadet emerged from hiding, calling his name.

Zare recognized Dev's voice and raised his faceplate.

"You're a stealthy one, Dev Morgan," he said.

Dev looked a bit embarrassed, and Zare was tempted to tell him that it was okay—he didn't have to keep hiding behind a name they both knew was fake. But it was entertaining to watch Dev squirm.

"Yeah, that's me—stealthy Dev Morgan," he said. "Hey, thanks for meeting me last minute, cadet. By the way, how'd you get past the gate?"

"I've been promoted," Zare said. "Got class-three clearance now."

"Um, congratulations?"

"To both of us. New clerical and courier duties give me greater access to intel you can use."

Dev ducked back behind the crates as several stormtroopers walked past the mouth of the alley. Zare waited until they had passed, then exhaled gratefully.

"Unless I'm caught, in which case . . ."

"Yeah, let's not get you shot," Dev said. "What do you have?"

Zare thought back to what he'd been able to discover in the Imperial files with his new clearance, wondering briefly what Merei could have obtained with her own forged credentials. But that wasn't possible anymore.

"Agent Kallus and every section commander have been in secret tactical meetings," he told Dev. "He's gathering troops for a massive operation."

Dev looked grave. "Any idea what for?"

"Something to do with the old Senate Building," Zare said. "But it might just be a drill. I'm not sure."

"It's no drill," Dev said grimly. "I need to warn the others."

He turned to go, but Zare stopped him. "Hey, one more thing—I'm being transferred off-world, to the officers' academy on Arkanis."

Dev paused, then turned to face Zare.

"There's something you should know," he said.

"Don't tell me you're gonna miss me, Dev," Zare said.

The look on Dev's face convinced Zare to keep up the charade as long as possible.

"What?" Dev stammered. "No . . . I mean, sure. But . . . look, that's not it. My real name is not Dev."

Zare thought he did a good job of looking surprised. "It's not your name?"

"No, it's—"

"You there!" said a harsh filtered voice.

Stormtroopers were coming down the alley behind Dev.

Dev said something Zare didn't quite catch—he thought he heard something about a vision—then turned toward Zare, flipping his faceplate down.

"No time to explain!" he muttered, then elbowed Zare hard in the chest. Zare fell to the ground as Dev raced off into the maze of alleyways.

A stormtrooper stopped as Zare got to his feet.

"Cadet, you all right?" he asked.

"Yes, sir," Zare said. "I . . . caught that Loth-rat selling black-market goods."

He joined in as the stormtroopers clattered down the alley, pursuing Dev. They chased him through the warren of small streets but lost him—to Zare's relief.

Zare followed the stormtroopers back toward the plaza. As they emerged, though, he caught sight of movement in the shadows. Zare paused as the troopers continued their search, then slipped back into the alley. Had Dev doubled back to find him again? Did he need something else?

A barrel fell over, the clang echoing through the alley. But the boy who stepped out into the narrow shaft of moonlight wasn't Dev Morgan.

It was Oleg, wild-eyed and in civilian clothes.

"I saw you!" he screamed, fists raised. "You were with Morgan! You're a traitor, and I'm going to tell everybody!"

"And who's going to believe you?" Zare asked coldly, turning his back on Oleg. "You're a washout cadet who associates with criminals."

With a cry, the former cadet flung himself at Zare, who ducked and flung him over his shoulders. Oleg landed on his back with a grunt, then scrambled up and lunged at Zare again. Zare caught him by the neck and propelled him into the wall of a building, the impact driving the air out of Oleg's lungs. He kicked desperately at Zare, clawing at his arm in an effort to break his grip.

"You wanted an Empire of blind obedience to the law, without fear or favor," Zare said. "Remember? And you got your reward."

"Traitor," Oleg gasped, his shoulders sagging.

Zare pushed his face close to Oleg's.

"You have no idea what I am or what I'm capable of," he said. "But if I ever see you again, you'll find out."

He let go of Oleg, who fell to his knees and scrambled away on all fours, knocking over barrels and crates in his haste to escape. Zare watched him go, then emerged from the alleyway, brushing himself off.

A stormtrooper commander marched over to him.

"There are criminals everywhere in the market-place, sir," Zare said. "I'd suggest a full sweep to clean the riffraff out."

He fingered a rip in his tunic, face impassive. Oleg had deserved what he got. An Empire of Olegs would mean a brutal galaxy in which citizens' lives were ruled by terror.

So why did Zare feel like running home and hiding in his room? And why was he suddenly frightened to ask what he was becoming?

EPILOGUE

Merei woke up screaming again.

Her father was in her room in less than a minute, sitting on the side of her bed and bundling her into his arms.

"It's all right, Mer Bear," Gandr said, rocking her. "It's all right. He's dead, and you're safe."

Merei's hair was wet with sweat. She shoved it out of her eyes and took a ragged breath, reminding herself that her father was just trying to help. He couldn't understand that Laxo's being dead meant it wasn't all right, and might never be again.

She couldn't get back to sleep. None of them could.

They wound up in the kitchen before dawn, with Merei sipping warm tea while Jessa drank caf and Gandr opened the first of the many fizzy Moogan teas he consumed each day.

"Think I'll finish up my closing report about the Transportation Ministry breach," Jessa said.

"Good idea," Gandr said, turning to Merei. "You saved your mother some work, at least. Locking down and searching three repeater services would have been tedious, to say the least."

"Not funny," Jessa said.

"You're right," Gandr said, gulping tea. "Sorry."

"So your investigation's over, Mom?" Merei asked.

"I wanted to finish the job, but I was overruled," Jessa said. "I don't doubt that this Gray Syndicate was behind the breach—your testimony about the kidnapping and what they said in the speeder van was evidence enough. But establishing the site the intrusion was launched from would have given us a more complete picture of the group's operation, in case the strike team didn't get it all. But the Empire has bigger priorities now—such as new security screening for commercial transport. So yes, the investigation's over."

Merei nodded, resisting the urge to close her eyes.

She feared she'd see Laxo's face again, the look of bafflement and betrayal.

"Your datapad's pinging, Mer Bear," her father said.

"At this hour?" Jessa asked.

Merei hurried up the stairs. Her datapad had fallen silent, but the message indicator was on. She tapped the screen and Zare appeared, sitting in one of the little rooms the cadets were allowed to use three days a week.

This isn't an approved comm time, she thought.

"Hey, Merei," Zare said, looking nervous. "I hope you weren't asleep. I . . . I've been going crazy trying to figure out how not to mess this message up, and now I probably will anyway. But I'm out of time. It's now or never.

"So, I'm being transferred to Arkanis," he said, and Merei's hand flew up to her mouth. "Which means I'm closer to my goal, the one we worked for together."

He looked at the cam unit and smiled, but his eyes were sad.

"I just . . . I'm so sorry for everything that went wrong between us," he said. "No, that's not right. I'm sorry for messing up everything we had. I wanted to tell you that I know everything you did to get me to this point. Along with everything it cost you. And . . . and I'm sorry for all the times I was too wrapped up in myself to remember that."

He stopped for a moment, catching his breath, then stared into the cam unit.

"Now I'm going where I need to be," Zare said. "And I'll succeed in what we worked for. No matter what it takes."

And then he was gone.

Merei stared at the screen for a long moment, thinking of what her mother had said: that the investigation was over, that the Empire had other priorities now.

Before she could talk herself out of it, she'd shoved the datapad aside and woken up her network terminal, fingers flying over the keys in familiar patterns. She activated the encryption protocol Jix had shared with her and bounced her message request through multiple repeater services. Then she stared at the screen for a moment.

"Well, come on, then," she muttered.

She called up her old Imperial Security Bureau account, entered her credentials, and waited for a warning that the account no longer existed.

But it was still there. She was in. She wasn't sure if she was glad about that or not.

Merei navigated to the Academy database and entered Zare's name. The most recent document in his file was titled TRANSFER.

She opened it.

IMMEDIATE TRANSFER TO ARKANIS APPROVED PER
INQUISITOR'S ORDERS RE PROJECT HARVESTER AND
MORGAN INVESTIGATION.

Merei logged out and woke up her datapad, comming Zare. But he didn't respond.

She tried again.

Nothing.

She shut down her network terminal, then nearly fell over in her haste to get dressed.

"I need to get an early start," Merei called to her parents.

"But, Mer Bear—" Gandr said.

"You just told me I was safe, remember?" Merei said, patting her jacket pocket. "And I've got my locator."

She raced across the city on her jumpspeeder, cleaning dust from her goggles while stopped at traffic signals; a brisk wind had been driving dust from the Westhills over the city all week. After she identified herself, Auntie Nags asked what her business was, and Merei could imagine the old nanny droid's photoreceptors flashing red. Then there was chatter over the speaker, and she was allowed up.

"Merei, it's nice to see you," said Tepha, folding the girl in her arms. Merei clung to Zare's mother for a long moment, chest heaving.

"You must have heard about Zare," Leo said from the kitchen table. "Arkanis! A midyear transfer, no less! Isn't it wonderful?"

Merei nodded and smiled, but Tepha was already getting her coat.

"The ladies are going for a walk," she told her husband, then turned to Merei when they were just steps away from the apartment, expression grave.

"They're not transferring Zare to Arkanis as a reward," Merei said. "They moved him there because of Dhara—and because they think he's connected to the insurgent group that made the recent rebel transmission. They sent Zare to Arkanis to break him and discover everything he knows."

Tepha clutched at Merei, who worried Zare's mother might collapse.

"Then he'll never come back from that awful place," Tepha whispered. "I've lost my daughter, and now my son is gone, too."

Merei and Tepha clung together in the cold for a long time, as the wind whipped at their coats and filled their hair with dust.

ABOUT THE AUTHOR

Jason Fry is the author of *The Jupiter Pirates* young-adult space-fantasy series and has written or co-written some two dozen novels, short stories, and other works set in the galaxy far, far away, including *The Essential Atlas* and *The Clone Wars Episode Guide*. He lives in Brooklyn, New York, with his wife, son, and about a metric ton of *Star Wars* stuff.